# The Boxer

# The Boxer

## Mike Tucker

outskirtspress

DENVER, COLORADO

The Boxer
All Rights Reserved.
Copyright © 2014 Mike Tucker
v2.0

Outskirts Press, Inc.
http://www.outskirtspress.com

ISBN: 978-1-4787-2438-4

Library of Congress Control Number: 2013919281

Outskirts Press and the "OP" logo are trademarks belonging to Outskirts Press, Inc.

PRINTED IN THE UNITED STATES OF AMERICA

# PRAISE FOR MIKE TUCKER

"Tucker's characters are unforgettable and he develops them all through their insightful and down-to-earth dialogues [in *1931*]."
**Karen Pirnot, *Readers Favorite*,**
**www.barnesandnoble.com**

"Point-blank, provocative and raw, a tour de force of narrative, *1931* is Mike Tucker's best novel, his most unique and distinctive work-- authentic and compelling."
**Will Layman, American jazz critic,**
**author and educator**

"I loved *Spartacus Did the Right Thing*. Bravo, Mike Tucker."
**Greg Craig, former White House Counsel to**
**President Obama and attorney-at-law**

"*RONIN*, by Mike Tucker, a gripping book on Marine snipers in Iraq, is along with *Ghost Wars*, one of the top ten books since September 11th."
**Matt LaPlante, Foreign correspondent,**
***THE SALT LAKE TRIBUNE***

"Mike Tucker— Hemingway is back. *Hell Is Over:* 5 stars."
**Mark Hastings, www.amazon.com**

"In *Hell Is Over*, Mike Tucker tells a story that we should know but would not, except for his courage."
**Bob Kerrey, former US Senator
and US Navy SEAL commander**

"If Hemingway were alive, he would be buying drinks for Mike Tucker all night long, for Tucker's vivid, moving first-hand account of a 250 kilometer deep reconnaissance behind Burmese Army lines, *The Long Patrol*, pivots on those quintessentially Hemingwayesque themes of armed men fighting to survive against overwhelming odds, and simply battling against the elements. Outstanding."
**Jim Algie, Editor, author and journalist.
*Untamed Travel.***

# BOOKS BY MIKE TUCKER

Fiction

**The Boxer**
**1931**
**Spartacus Did the Right Thing**
**African Skies**

Non-Fiction

**Hell Is Over**
**Taking Down Al Qaeda In the Hindu Kush**
**RONIN**
**The Long Patrol**
**Bring the Heat**
**Among Warriors in Iraq**
**Operation Hotel California**

*This book is dedicated in memory of the great Welsh poet Dylan Thomas (1914-1953), and Geoffrey Morley-Mower (1918-2005), Royal Air Force wing commander and a brilliant reconnaissance pilot in the Second World War – poet, mentor and friend.*

"Everything leads to something beyond."

**Ruth Mallory**

# The Boxer

Nothing comes at you harder than life. The priest thought about that now, listening to a Christmas carol from a radio in a diner in the small mountain town of Chinle, Northern Arizona, a little after eight in the evening on December 18, 2012. He could see McCullough stepping away from a heavy bag a long time passing, sweat pouring down his face, "Nothing comes at you harder than life, buddy, and God helps those who help themselves — but you knew that."

Jesse McCullough, orphaned when he was five months old and a boxer all his life, the priest reflected. Maybe he can help the kid. You couldn't. You and every psychologist in Northern Arizona couldn't.

"It's a rough thing for a kid to go through," the priest said now, looking at a couple across from him in a booth of the diner. He drank coffee from a white porcelain cup and set the cup down on a table between them.

The priest's name was Father James Youngblood. He had dark eyes and salt-and-pepper hair. A thin red scar ran jagged over his right eyebrow. He was wearing brown leather cowboy boots, a black collared shirt, blue jeans and a black leather jacket. In the way of some priests, he was married before he'd taken on the calling. A lean man and a little over six feet tall, he had been a hunting guide in the American Southwest and Africa before entering Catholic seminary in Kentucky in 2002, when he was forty-four.

There was a buzz from his cell phone now and the priest lifted the small black cell phone out of his jacket. Touching the keypad, he could see a text message from his wife, "Caveman:) Get milk&eggs. xxxooo, Becky." He set his cell phone back in his jacket, looking at the couple again and feeling butterflies in his gut. You are *their* priest, he thought now, and you can't fail them but damn it.

"Rough thing for anyone to go through," the priest said, going on, taking a sip from his coffee. "Everyone loved Billy. For a kid to die like that, from a brain aneurysm, just taken away in a heartbeat. I'll tell you what, I have no idea how that must feel for a child to lose a good friend like that, I really don't. And Tommy, well he felt the pain nearly as much as Billy's kin. I feel terrible that I've failed you all. God help me, I just couldn't get through to Tommy. And I know these last five weeks have been hard for you all. But it's Christmas and in a week, Tommy will be opening presents under the tree and maybe there will be a smile on his face and maybe there won't, but at least you've still got a son," his voice nearly breaking.

The priest made the Sign of the Cross, looking at the young mother and father across from him and thinking of every mother and father who has ever lost a child and every child who has ever lost a friend. He had quit smoking when he became a priest and he was thinking as he drank coffee now that he damn sure needed a smoke to cool him out. He wiped tears from his eyes and took a deep breath, pulling himself together.

"There are twenty-six families in New England right now," the priest said softly, setting his coffee down, "who are looking at Christmas presents that will never be opened."

He was thinking of the children and teachers massacred at Sandy Hook Elementary School in Newtown, Connecticut four days before and he remembered now that he'd been with his wife when he'd heard the news of the first graders gunned down in their classrooms at Sandy Hook. He could still see his wife clutching her chest and crying and reaching out for him in the stone-floored kitchen of their adobe house in Chinle.

Looking out at the mountains in the night, the priest prayed a Hail Mary in his heart and looked back at the couple across from him.

"And I'm sorry," he said, laying his palms out toward them, "I came here to tell you there's one last way that I think might help Tommy but I can't get those kids' faces out of my mind. I'm sorry. And I wish I could tell you for sure that Jesse McCullough can make a difference for Tommy, I wish I could tell you that. But I can't. I can't promise you a blessed thing. All I can tell you is that I know that Jesse has made a difference in a lot of kids' lives. He's been a boxer all his life and he's helped a lot of orphans — he knows how to reach kids and he knows how to listen to kids. He got through to a kid last week, helped him tremendously, a thirteen year old kid who'd been bullied at school and was just down on himself and down on the world. The boy's parents had done all they could since last spring. They came to Jesse and in about ten minutes, he got through to the kid. I know how impossible that sounds but it's true. Sometimes nothing is stranger than the truth. I can't explain how Jesse got through to that kid, neither could Jesse when I talked to him about it, there's no logical reason why Jesse was able to help the kid that solid and that quick, but that's the thing about the truth, sometimes there's no logic to the truth. And that young man has turned the corner, thank God."

The man sitting across from the priest looked down, nodding his head briefly, his rough, calloused hands folded together.

His name was Cole Benson and he was twenty-five that winter. Cole was a big, slope-shouldered man with green eyes and dark hair who'd lived in Chinle all his life. He was wearing a khaki-colored rancher's coat and a wool-lined red flannel work shirt and stained, faded blue jeans. Grains of sand and gray pebbled flecks of dried concrete were on his steel-toed brown leather work boots. He glanced up at the priest and there was a look of resignation just shy of despair in Cole's eyes now.

You've known Father James since you first started working in concrete, Cole thought, taking a sip from his coffee. Always on the level, always straight from the shoulder. Tommy was just born. My Lord, where does the time go. He's right, Cole thought, a reflective look come over him, we've got a helluva' lot to be grateful for. Setting his coffee cup down, he touched a hand to his forehead, thinking of a funeral he'd watched on television earlier that day. There was a young woman in a long black overcoat and her brown hair was in a ponytail and she looked about the same age as his wife, he remembered now. And she was shaking and a man next to her who looked about his age was holding her and tears were pouring down their faces as they had buried their daughter in the snow in Newtown, Connecticut.

After a spell Cole glanced up, looking out the window at tall pines and snow on distant peaks and stars glittering in the darkness and he could see his son Tommy in his mind's eye, crying at the funeral of his son's best friend, Billy Uriah, on November 14, 2012 in Chinle. One day your son is wearing a Batman T-shirt and laughing and playing with his friends and asking you where does the moon go in the middle of the day and the next day he's asking you where is God, Cole thought.

Putting an arm around his shoulder, his wife looked him in his eyes, saying, "Cole, Tommy just looks more lonesome every time he sees another psychologist. Every time we ride back from one of those counseling sessions, he just sits in the back seat and doesn't say a word. Padre," she said, nodding to the priest now, "you don't have to be sorry for anything. We cried too, when we heard about the massacre in Newtown. It's our worst nightmare, losing our son the way those folks lost their children. I can't even begin to imagine what they are going through. But Padre, we just want to see Tommy smile again. Just see him smile, he was always so happy-go-lucky before. Now he leaves for school every day like he's got the weight of the world on his shoulders."

Vickie Benson wiped a tear from the corner of an eye. She drank coffee slowly, looking at the priest and holding her husband's hand. She was twenty-four that winter and her hair was long and black, falling over her red and purple wool blanket coat. She was wearing faded blue jeans and a dark blue cotton sweater and black leather boots. Turquoise and silver earrings that had been in her family for seven generations hung from her ears and she had high cheekbones and coal-black eyes.

Vickie glanced out at the stars in the night now and set her coffee cup down on the table. She looked at Cole and he could feel her dark eyes kind on him and he squeezed her hand gently.

"Maybe the padre is right, Cole. Maybe we should give Mr. McCullough a chance," she said, looking at Cole.

"Vickie," he said softly, looking in her eyes.

"Father James, you've got a big heart," he said now, turning and reaching a hand across the table. "And I want you to know something," he said, going on, drinking coffee and looking the priest in his eyes.

"You've always been there for us, you've always been there for my family. Don't you ever feel like you failed us. You're a true priest, true man of God. But Padre, on my wages—I can't do this. Even with Vickie's take-home from the grocery store. You're talking boxing. That means money. It's winter, we don't pour concrete in the winter. I'm a foreman now and running a crew but money is money and we'll be off this winter, next ten weeks, right up to March 1st. I've been on unemployment since the tenth of this month. Happens every winter but this year just seems tougher, tougher to stay on top of our bills and tougher to save for Tommy's college. Being away from home, working the contracts in Flagstaff this year, well, that didn't help my family, either. Bottom-line, Padre, I'm not going to cut into the monthly savings for Tommy's college, I'm not going to cut into his college money. My father had a saying, "A man never goes back on his word." Well, I gave my word to Vickie, we swore an oath together that we would never touch that money. And I'll damn well keep that oath—that college fund is Tommy's future, God willing. So I don't see how we can do this, I just don't. If I had champagne money, no worries, even whiskey money would do but I'm a few dollars short of beer money right now. Uncle Hank, great uncle of mine from Santa Fe, he was a boxer. Damn good light heavyweight, too. Eighty years old now and still shadow boxes, still skips rope. But boxing, you're talking gym time, gloves, jump rope, headgear, workout gear — "

" — Jesse said he'd train Tommy for free," the priest said, gesturing to him.

Cole leaned forward, his eyebrows raised, looking at the priest.

"For real?"

"For real," the priest replied, his eyes cheerful. "*Absolutamonde. Gratis*, no worries. No strings attached. I even offered to pony up a stipend from the State of Arizona, special psychological counseling dispensation. Jesse said no dice, he knows your situation. He was a concrete laborer himself, little over two decades ago. Worked concrete in Flagstaff, as he put it, "Back in the Stone Ages, back when I had more hair and less peace of mind and you, padre, were not wearing a black suit to work." All good, Cole. Money's not an issue."

Vickie smiled now, her eyes lighting up, drinking coffee. "Father James, thank you," she said as Cole, squinting, his lips pursed, incredulous, stared at the priest. "Cole," she said softly now, looking at her husband, "We can make it, baby. Between your unemployment this winter and what I bring home, we won't have to touch Tommy's college fund. Maybe this will help Tommy. I *told* you the padre could help us."

Cole smiled, looking in her eyes.

He grabbed his coffee cup and took a gulp from it and set it down, saying a prayer in his heart for his son. Holding his wife's hand, he looked at the priest now.

"Tell me about him."

The priest leaned forward, his elbows propped up on the table and his hands clasped, looking at Cole.

"Forty-three this year. His mother was a prostitute and a heroin addict. She left him at an orphanage in Flagstaff when he was five months old. Cops found her dead with a needle in her arm in an alley in Phoenix a year later."

"Lord have mercy," Cole said, a grim look come over him. "Did he ever find his father?"

The priest shook his head.

"No, his mother just had *John Doe* written on the birth certificate. I remember one time Jesse talked about his father. Jesse pointed to a heavy bag, smiled and said, "Buddy, *that's* my father. I was raised by a heavy bag and chopping wood and push-ups on my fists and the priests and nuns in Flagstaff, thank God for the orphanage." I'll tell you what, it made me think how blessed I was to have a father, growing up."

Cole nodded, drinking coffee and thinking of his own father in Chinle and remembering learning how to mix and pour concrete when he was eight years old, his father and his grandfather by his side, working with him all day under high blue mountain skies in Northern Arizona. He could still taste the lemonade they drank in the middle of that day in the summer of 1995, nothing sweeter or colder he'd ever drank since. He could still see his father taking a knee, telling him to take it easy, showing him how to tamp down the dirt and level it, taking a long wooden plane out and teaching him how to level a patch of dirt before pouring concrete that would be a sidewalk for a family by the end of the day. Mercy you were lucky. Man how do you grow up without a father, my God, and you lose your mother when you're five months old. Jesse damn sure overcame a world of hurt. And the world didn't break him. The world did everything it could to break him and he never broke, mercy. No mother and no father and he must have felt like the world was a very lonely place, when he was old enough to feel. And that's pretty damn young, when you're old enough to feel that kind of pain. But he found a way to carry on, Cole reflected, looking at the priest, he damn sure found a way to carry on.

"When did he start boxing?"

"Seven years old. Fought Golden Gloves in his teens."

"Seven? Little young to be in the ring, Padre."

"Shadow-boxing, footwork, roadwork, speed bag and light work on the heavy bag. You're right, it's pretty young to be learning how to fight. Worked out good for Jesse, though. Seventeen when he started working as a concrete laborer. Got married at eighteen. Not enough steak in the icebox, is what he told me about his divorce. Volunteered for the US Army Rangers in 1988. That's where I met him."

"You were a Ranger?," Cole asked in a calm, no-nonsense tone, looking at him.

The priest nodded.

"I got out in October '89. My last year, I was in the same platoon as Jesse."

"Is he still a Ranger?," Vickie asked.

"No," the priest said, shaking his head, a sober look come over him. Drinking coffee, he looked back at them and set his cup down slowly on the table. God hates liars and cowards, the priest thought now. You are their priest and you can't lie to them, Tommy is their son and it's their call. Last thing Jesse would want is for you to sugarcoat it. All right then. Straight, no chaser.

"He's a mercenary," the priest said, not losing their eyes.

Vickie put a hand over her mouth and Cole glanced quickly at her.

Cole looked hard at the priest.

"You *want* a mercenary to help Tommy get his head straight?," Cole said, shaking his head, eyeballing the priest. "For Chrissakes, what'd you smoke for breakfast, Padre?"

Vickie reached out and held her husband's hands, her brow furrowed, glancing down briefly. She whispered in his ear. Cole shrugged and said to her, "Go ahead."

"Father James, you have been a rock for us," she said, looking the priest in his eyes. "You have tried to help Tommy in every way. We appreciate everything you've done for us, we really do. But a mercenary? Mr. McCullough kills people for a living, right? I mean, sweet Jesus, he *kills* people for a living. And you think he can help Tommy? How can he help my little boy, what can he teach him, what does he know? There must be someone else we can reach out to, there's gotta' be somebody else. Padre, for God's sakes, he's a *mercenary*."

The priest nodded, squinting, not looking away.

"And he's the best man I know," the priest said, looking calmly at her. "I was paid to kill people, too, if you want to put it that way, when I was a Ranger. I killed terrorists and I got paid for it on active duty in the Rangers. So did Jesse. Jesse still kills terrorists, he just doesn't have an American flag on his right shoulder anymore. Look, I *trained* Jesse. All I know is that there's no one else I can reach out to that can help Tommy, no one. And I'll tell you what Jesse McCullough can teach Tommy. He can teach him how to take the pain and carry on. He can teach him to never take one step backwards. He can teach him how to defend others and defend himself. And he can teach him how to save his own life. Now those are all good reasons he can help Tommy, but there are over 25,000 more reasons you ought to give Jesse a chance, and all of them damn fine."

Cole folded his arms across his chest.

"25,000 *what?*," Cole said, staring at the priest.

"25,000 lives saved. And more. That's what. That's how many lives Jesse saved in 2008. For that alone, you ought to seriously consider giving him a shot at helping Tommy. A man who knows how to save lives is a man worth listening to."

Cole leaned back, his arms still folded, looking at the priest. Vickie whispered in his ear and he wrapped an arm around her shoulders. He nodded to the priest now, as if to say go ahead.

"Jesse McCullough stopped seventeen Al Qaeda suicide bomb teams that year," the priest said slowly.

Cole realized he'd never seen the priest look as serious as he did right now, eyes like two line drives, Cole was thinking as the priest went on.

"He wasn't alone on those missions but he was on point."

"Where?," Cole asked quickly, sitting bolt upright now as Vickie leaned forward.

"Sumatra, Indonesia. Malaysia and Singapore. Strait of Malacca. On shore and at high sea. Took down Al Qaeda — Al Qaeda, and Jemma E Islamiyah terrorists out of Sumatra, Malaysia and Indonesia. They were targeting the heart of Kuala Lumpur, Malaysia, and a few other places. Al Qaeda and Jemma E Islamiyah suicide bomb assaults on land and at high sea. Jesse and his team stopped them dead in their tracks."

"My Lord," Vickie said softly and she squeezed Cole's hand.

Father James raised a hand now toward a waitress with a long black ponytail, a young lady in blue jeans and a gray wool sweater, who was standing near the counter of the diner, sending a text message on her cell phone to her boyfriend. She caught his eye and nodded quickly to the priest and set her cell phone in a sweater pocket.

The waitress grabbed a hot, fresh pot of black coffee from behind the counter and came over and re-filled their coffee cups, the priest saying to her, "Merry Christmas, Ruby. Please tell your father that Becky and I hope he gets that job cross-town."

"Merry Christmas, Padre," she said, nodding to him and smiling and glancing at Cole and Vickie now. "My Dad will be glad to hear that, we all appreciate that. You know, it'd be great to see him working on motorcycles again, it really would. He loves that work. Thank you," holding the coffee pot steady in her right hand and flipping the black plastic top of the pot shut with her left hand.

"How is Tommy doing?," she said, looking at Vickie.

"He's hanging in there," Vickie said.

"We're all praying for him," Ruby said. "It's so hard to lose a friend, especially at that age."

"That's so kind of you, Ruby," Vickie said, looking at her and smiling. "That really means a lot to us. God bless you."

"Merry Christmas, Ruby," Cole said, looking at her and smiling as he held Vickie's hand. "Much obliged."

Ruby nodded to them, her eyes warm and peaceful as a bell chimed from the front door of the diner.

Grinning, she said quickly to them, "Merry Christmas," hustling back across the diner. A stocky, heavily-built man with blonde hair and a beard, in carpenter's jeans and a sand-colored canvas work coat and dusty, scuffed brown leather work boots, sat up on a stool at the counter now. He laid a black wool watch cap down on the counter, rubbing his hands warm.

"But it's like both of you told me here the other

night," the priest said now, drinking coffee and glancing out at the stars in the darkness before looking back at Cole and Vickie.

"Go ahead, Padre," Cole said, drinking coffee, looking him in his eyes.

"Tommy is hurting," the priest said, setting his coffee cup down on the table. "He's hurting in a place that only he knows and he's not letting anyone in. He's put up a wall between him and the world. That wall is a hundred miles deep and a hundred miles wide and it scares the living hell out of me. And I know where it leads. There's no good there, at the end of that line, no damn good at all. What really troubles me is that you've had nearly every psychologist in Northern Arizona try to help him. And they didn't make a dent. Truth, it scares the hell out of Becky. Not a coffee we drink every morning goes by without her talking about Tommy, not a whiskey we drink in the evening, not a night goes by without her lighting a candle in a window and saying a prayer for Tommy. I think grief is blinding Tommy's heart—a Jesuit priest told me something at seminary in Kentucky ten years ago that really rocked me: "'There is beauty all around us but in grief, it's easy to miss that beauty. Grief blinds the heart. When the heart is blinded by grief, nothing reaches the soul, not all the beauty in the world, not the beauty in a sunrise or a flower or a child's smile.

And when someone is in grief, you must grieve with them, if you are going to have a chance at helping them. Everybody suffers but not everybody heals. I think it is true that God helps those who help themselves, yes. But I know something real about helping people. I know that you can make a difference in this world. Sometimes a man finds that he is in exactly the right place at exactly the right time to help someone on this earth. I have seen that happen in the lives of many people and of course, I cannot explain it. But when it happens, one realizes that destiny is as mysterious as God." Well, I had to give a sermon that week at seminary and I gave it based on what he'd told me."

Vickie held Cole's hand now and she looked at the priest.

"Do you still remember that sermon, Padre?," she asked him, looking quickly at Cole now and Cole nodded to her, slipping his hand out from under her hand and wrapping an arm around her shoulder.

The priest looked at her and nodded. He drank coffee and said softly, "I sure do." He closed his eyes and prayed a Hail Mary in his heart now for Tommy and opening his eyes, he looked at them.

"To reach people in grief," the priest said, "you've got to have a listening heart. And your actions must say, in the way of Christ: *Walk with me,*

*grieve with me, lean on me and I will help you carry on.*
Because we are all on a hard journey in this life.
And it's beauty, and ultimately love, that sustains
us and helps us deal with grief. Sometimes life
is nothing but pain. And nothing heals like love.
Christ believed in love. A love that heals grief, a
love that touches the hearts of people in grief, a
love that sustains people in moments of doubt and
despair. And too, a love that celebrates being alive,
a love that speaks forever about being grateful for
each sunrise, being grateful for being alive, being grateful for our friends and loved ones. Love
heals. Christ understood that. When Christ says
to us to help widows and orphans, He is saying
more than pray for them, because they are people
in need. And of course we pray for all people in
need, but it's our actions that define us. He is saying give them charity, give them food and shelter
and compassion. Give them love. People in need
are people who need love more than anything else
and we are all people in need. And when Christ
stood with that woman in the dust who was staring into death and shared her pain, stood down
that mob that wanted to end her days, He defined
courage, and love. Forever. What Christ said to
that woman, in His actions, was simply one of the
most caring, most generous, and truly most loving
things: *You are not alone, I will face death with you*

*and I will never abandon you.* People in grief need to feel in their heart and soul and bone marrow that they are not alone. They need to feel that they are not abandoned. And all I really know about reaching out to people in grief is that you must listen with your heart. You must listen to people in grief with a whole heart, a humble heart and above all, a listening heart. Without a listening heart, you cannot help anyone in this world."

Vickie smiled at him and Cole looked in his eyes and nodded to him as if to say, go on.

"You know," Father James said now, drinking coffee, "I learned more from that priest, whose name was Father Jeremiah and who died this past April, than I learned in all the months I was at seminary. And the main thing I can tell you about Jesse McCullough is that he has a listening heart. He really knows how to listen and that's more important here than anything else. Some folks are born with that trait, some folks learn it, but wherever he got it, he got a lot of it. God protect Tommy. I swear I've done everything I could and I came up short. I thought about you all long and hard the last few days. And it hit me like a landslide yesterday, maybe Jesse can help."

Cole gestured as if to say, wait a minute, and whispered in his wife's ear and she kissed him on a cheek.

"When can Tommy start?," Cole said, looking at the priest now.

The priest smiled, his eyes brightening. He fished his cell phone out from his jacket.

"I was hoping you'd say that," the priest said. "I gave Jesse a holler yesterday. He told me Tommy could start training on the 22nd, if that suits Tommy and that suits you all."

"It's up to Tommy. And if the General says OK, then I reckon it should be OK. What do you think about the 22nd, General," Cole said, grinning, looking in Vickie's eyes.

"We'll know once we talk to Tommy but it sounds fine to me," she said, smiling and wrapping an arm around his waist. "This damn fool I call my husband started calling me the General last week, Padre. Said that I'm always in command. I told him if that's so then he can salute me every time I fix him a cup of coffee."

"And every time he buys you a new set of heels," the priest said, grinning.

"That'd be mighty fine, too," she said, pinching Cole. He kissed her on a cheek, smiling.

"Absolutely. Padre, is Mr. McCullough in Arizona right now?," Cole asked, drinking the last of his coffee. The priest shook his head, a wry smile on his face.

"Been a long time since he was in Arizona, Cole.

Jesse lives in Penang, Malaysia. Northern Strait of Malacca."

Cole whistled, his eyebrows raised.

"Padre, that's on the other side of the *world.* "

The priest nodded to him, zipping up his jacket.

"That's right, little south of Bangkok and a little north of Singapore. No worries, Jesse told me he'd fly into Flagstaff, morning of the 20th, if you all want his help. There's a cabin about seven miles north of here where Jesse would stay. He'd be bringing up the gear and equipment from Flagstaff on the 21st; a carpenter in town is going to help him. If Tommy wants to train, call me tonight with sizes for Tommy's boots, wool watch cap, gloves, socks, sweatshirts and sweatpants, and ballpark size on a nylon jacket for Tommy. Jesse would get all that for Tommy in Flagstaff, of course. Outstanding mountain cabin, two fireplaces inside and a fire pit facing west, outside. Jesse's renting the cabin from the McClure family in Tucson—"

"—Doc McClure, the stone mason?"

The priest nodded, saying, "You know him?"

Cole smiled, looking quickly at Vickie and nodding to the priest.

"Doc McClure, I'll be damned. Worked with him on a job in Flagstaff when I was a concrete laborer, five years ago."

"I'll tell you what, Doc built the fireplaces in

that cabin north of here, and a stone porch, looking out west," the priest said. "You know, Doc's
given a lot of charity to a lot of different churches
in Arizona, he's helped build a few churches for
free. And a few Buddhist temples. By the way, Doc
asked me to tell you that he and his family, and the
folks at his church, St. Luke's in Tucson, are praying for Tommy, night and day."

"Please give him our thanks, Padre, and please
tell Mr. McClure that we wish his family and everyone at St. Luke's a very Merry Christmas and
a very happy New Year," Vickie said softly now,
looking at the priest. Cole nodded to her, holding
her hand.

"If Tommy agrees to this, honey, let's do this,"
Vickie said quickly now, looking in her husband's
eyes and he smiled and kissed her on a cheek.
"Padre, we'll call you tonight, after we talk to
Tommy," she said as Cole reached out a hand to
the priest.

Triangle-shaped pieces of dark brown leather,
with small shoulder patch flags from different
countries stitched on them, were tied to a porch
rail of a mountain cabin northwest of Chinle three
days before Christmas that winter. Sharp, piercing
rays of sunlight, strong mountain sun, glinted off
glass beads embossed on the leather. There was an

American flag flapping in the breeze near the stone and wood cabin in the mountains, the flag tied to a white-painted steel pole in front of the cabin, pine needles loose and thick near the concrete base of the pole. It was clear and cold in the mountains and you could see red and gold cliffs northwest of the cabin. There was snow on the cliffs and old packhorse and logging trails snaked near the cliffs on far ridgelines and the mountains were stark and beautiful and you could see snow shining white from peaks far to the north of the cabin.

About a hundred yards downhill from the cabin, near an old packhorse trail that snaked along a ridgeline studded with pine trees and oak trees and sycamore trees, Jesse McCullough was chopping wood when he saw the priest's silver pickup truck coming around a snowy bend in a jeep trail, coming toward the cabin in the mountains a little past three in the afternoon on December 22, 2012. A midnight blue pick-up was roughly thirty yards behind the priest's vehicle now, coming up the mountain through the snow.

Jesse waved to them, smiling, a black and green wool scarf wrapped around his neck. He was 5' 10" and barrel-chested, a natural middleweight in his youth. A scar from a bullet wound splotched out in a small, quarter-sized circle on his right forearm. Two decades and change of wearing a flak jacket and carrying weapons, rounds, grenades, rations and water on three continents had built him up to about 180 pounds. His eyes were dark and his short-cropped hair was silver and he had the dark golden tan of someone who has spent a lifetime in the tropics. He was wearing a gray hooded sweatshirt over a black wool turtleneck. His gray sweatpants fell loosely over custom-made black leather and green canvas jungle boots that had not much black left on them. Lightweight green wool gloves on his hands edged out from under thick black leather work gloves. A pair of black leather fighting gloves, with the fingertips cut off in the MMA style, were lashed together with long brown leather laces and slung over a branch on a pine tree near him.

A large, faded, olive green canvas duffel bag leaned against an oak tree behind him, filled with training gear and workout clothes for Tommy: Two gray hooded sweatshirts and two crew neck sweatshirts, a navy blue wool turtleneck, a pair of running shoes and a pair of brown leather work boots, wool-lined brown leather work gloves, two black wool watch caps, two navy blue wool scarves, six pairs each of wool socks and cotton socks, two lightweight polypro turtleneck jerseys, two pairs of black leather fighting gloves and two pairs of lightweight green wool gloves.

A medical kit in a black leather satchel—filled with khaki-colored, soft surgical tape, band aids, liniment, betadine, antibiotic gel, cotton swabs, q-tips, a jar of Vaseline and a bottle of mineral oil, rubbing alcohol, aspirin, ibuprofen, vitamins, fish oil, kelp supplements and amino acid supplements—was propped up against the duffle bag. Two large stainless steel thermoses, one painted black and holding coffee, the other unpainted and silver and filled with hot chocolate, sat atop a chunk of pine, near the satchel.

A black leather heavy bag, wrapped with gray duct tape, was hanging from a steel hook rigged to a chain thrown over a long, thick branch of the oak tree near McCullough. The heavy bag was standard, in a tube shape, and weighed 225 pounds. Another black leather heavy bag, in a teardrop shape and weighing 200 pounds, was hanging from a steel hook rigged to a chain thrown over a lower branch of the same oak. Near each side of each chain, gray duct tape was taped thick around the branches, about six inches thick and taped an inch away from each side of each chain, the four thickly-taped rings of gray duct tape keeping the chains from sliding down the branches.

A pit was on the other side of the oak tree, dug about five feet deep and ten feet wide and ten feet long, lined with gravel. A wooden ladder was jammed into the pit. Wind-blown snow dusted the pit.

There were two piles of stones in the pit. There was enough room in the pit for two men to stand, back to back, tossing stones out of the pit. About ten yards south of the pit, a waterproofed, green canvas tarp lay on top of the snow, a few stones tossed on it to keep it from being blown away by the strong mountain winds that often come ripping through the hills in the late afternoon in the winters in Chinle.

A sandbox the size of a boxing ring, twenty feet by twenty feet, stood about ten yards north of the oak tree. The sandbox had been dug into the mountainside. Rough-hewn pine walled three sides of the sandbox and boulders walled in the fourth side.

A second, smaller sandbox, ten feet wide by ten feet long, was dug into the mountain-side twenty yards uphill from the sandbox boxing ring and walled with timber on all four sides. Four small concrete rods (steel rebar) were bent into horseshoe shapes and wedged into the sand, side by side, on the southern end of the small sandbox, the rebar just high enough for a man's feet to fit through. A man laying on his back with his feet through the horseshoe-shaped rebar could do crunches, with his hands behind his head and curling his body up, elbows touching his knees as he curled up from the sand. Jesse had been doing crunches earlier and left an impression on the sand in the pit, the shape of his back pressed back against the dark sand in the small pit.

You could see tall pines dusted with snow north of the boxer's cabin in the mountains. There were hawks gliding above the pines now and they flew toward snow-capped peaks northwest in the late afternoon. Hope the kid is ready to sweat, no better way to burn out the pain than sweating it out, McCullough thought now as the pick-up rolled to a stop about seventy yards uphill from McCullough.

Father James and the padre's wife, Becky, got out, her long blonde hair falling down her back.

Cole's midnight blue pick-up halted now and he set it in park and pulled up the emergency brake, saying to his son in the back seat, "Let's go, buddy."

McCullough reached down now and grabbed the thermos and opened it, poured out a half a cup of coffee and drank it slowly, waving again to Father James, Becky, Cole, Vickie and Tommy as they neared the cabin now.

They waved back to him and Cole said aloud, "You all walk on," and he looked at his wife and said, "Darlin', let's talk to Tommy for a spell."

Vickie stopped in the snow and nodded to Cole

and kissed him on a cheek as Father James and Becky glanced at them, Becky looking at Tommy and smiling and saying, "Now go on and have some fun, young man, looks like Mr. McCullough sure has laid out a good boxing camp for you! God bless you, Tommy."

Tommy nodded and waved to Becky and smiled at Father James as Vickie whispered to her husband, "I sure hope this works out," and he nodded to her and whispered, "Hell yes."

She kneeled and looked at Tommy now and hugged him and kissed him on a cheek, looking in his eyes and saying to him, "You listen closely to Mr. McCullough and keep that scarf around your neck. You do what he tells you to do, he's been a boxer all his life, honey. He's a tough man and he's a good man. Your daddy and I respect him a lot and we're glad he's come here, from a long way away."

"He came all the way from the other side of the world, Mom! He lives in the place with the bamboo and tigers and stuff. Dad told me last night that he came from Malaysia and I looked it up on my Google maps and he came from Penang, Malaysia. There's a lighthouse there on that island. And lots of beaches! Penang sure looks like a beautiful place, Mom. But it sure is far, I looked it up and it's a long, long way from us. About 9,000 miles! Mom, that sure is a long way."

"Yes it is," she said, smiling at her son and tousling his hair. "I love you, Tommy."

"Love you too, Mom," Tommy said softly, nodding to her. She stood up now and he reached out to his mother and father and they held his hands as he stood between them. "I get to hit the heavy bag now, like you and Dad told me!," he said, cockeyed-excited and smiling, making a fist with his right hand now and punching the air.

"That's right, Tommy!," Vickie said, looking in his eyes and thinking how beautiful it was to see her son smile again and saying a prayer in her heart for her son. "Now your Dad's gonna talk to you. I'll see you later, Tommy," and she smiled at him and patted her son on a shoulder and walked on up the mountain toward the cabin.

Cole took a knee in the snow, looking Tommy in his eyes now.

"Now you remember what I told you, buddy," Cole said, his eyes warm and cheerful, "Mr. McCullough served our country in the Rangers, long before you were born. He's a damned good man, he's stopped some real bad guys, for real. When you see Old Glory, I want you to never forget that Mr. McCullough and men like him, men like him and Father James, men like your granddad and your uncles, well pardner, they are the men who stand tall for us, for our people, and for

Old Glory. He's a man who's saved a lot of lives, and like Father James likes to say, "A man who knows how to save lives is a man worth listening to." So you need to listen to him, pardner. Like your mama told you, just do what he says. And he's from Northern Arizona, like you, pardner, like you and like everyone in our family. You listen to him real good and respect the hell out of him, because I damn sure do. And don't you be afraid to hit those heavy bags, looks like he's got two of them set up right nice for you, son."

"Yessir," Tommy said quickly, glancing at his father and grinning.

Tommy was about four feet tall and his thick black hair flared up from his head and his eyes were coal-black. He was six years old and wearing brown leather boots and beat-up khaki trousers and a gray nylon jacket over a red hooded sweatshirt, with a thick black wool scarf wrapped around his neck and black wool gloves on his hands. He had the sloped shoulders and deep-set eyes of his father and the high broad cheekbones of his mother, who was a full-blooded Navajo, like many of the people in Chinle.

"Good," his father said, standing up now and smiling at him and reaching a fist out toward Tommy and they touched fists in the snow. "Reckon I'll be up in the cabin. You have fun, pardner. You know that your Uncle Hank in Santa Fe was a damn fine light heavyweight, he was a fighter. He didn't start boxing until he was fourteen years old, so you're setting a new family record. How about that! You're making history in our family today, wild man. Got Uncle Hank beat by eight years! Didn't know when you woke up this morning that you'd be making history in the Benson family, did you?"

"Really?," Tommy said excitedly, his eyes bright, squinting. "Is that true about Uncle Hank, Dad? Uncle Hank was a boxer? I remember that you told me he is my great-great uncle. That makes Uncle Hank my double-great uncle! He is my double-great uncle. Maybe I'm the only kid at school with a double-great uncle who is still alive! I'll bet I am. Dad, you never told me that Uncle Hank was a boxer, you never told me that before."

"You never wanted to hit a heavy bag before," Cole said, smiling at his son. "Damn straight it's true, pardner. Golden Gloves champ he was, too. I'll tell you what, I believe you're gonna' sweat some, even in this cold. You go and have fun now. Couldn't be a more beautiful day, no doubt about it. I'll see you later, son."

Tommy nodded to him and said, "See you later, Dad," as Cole walked on uphill in the snow.

Looking downhill now, Tommy could see Jesse

McCullough raising an axe and splitting a chunk of pine, bark flying off the pine in the mountain snow.

Jesse reached out a hand to Tommy now and gestured toward two axes leaning up against the oak tree near them.

"You ready to chop some wood, Tommy?"

The boy looked around, at the mountains and the sky.

"I guess so, Mr. McCullough," he said now, looking at Jesse and shaking hands, a grin on the boy's face and a twinkle in his eyes. "I reckon I'm ready. Yessir. But I gotta' ask you a question. 'Cause my mom and dad told me that you are forty-three. So I gotta' ask you a question. Sir."

Jesse smiled at him.

"That's a madcap grin you're wearing, young man. I believe that you're gonna' ask me why my hair is all silver, aren't you, champ?"

Tommy smiled now, looking at him.

"Yessir," he said, folding his arms.

"Nearly as white as that old beard on Santa Claus, truth be told. Ol' Saint Nick, now, he's one of my uncles. That's how I got this white hair at my age, being related to him and what not. 'Gotta make sure I've got plenty of hay and oats for his reindeer, coming around this time of year, every

Christmas. Ol' Saint Nick ran out of red coats and trousers, don't you know, he told me I'd have to make do, that's why I've got these grey sweats. Merciful heaven. Call me Jesse."

Tommy grinned a sheepish grin now and Jesse grinned right back at him, shaking his head and thinking, man it is good to see him crack wise after all he's been through, good to see him smile. So he's got a little piss and vinegar in him, excellent, you sure had plenty of piss and vinegar in you when you were his age and wondering why every Mother's Day felt like hell and every Father's Day felt worse, days when you felt like the whole world hated you. Life was nothing but a world of hurt until you began hitting a heavy bag. Until that heavy bag became your father and mentor and brother protector and your best friend, ain't that the truth so help me God. Thank God for that heavy bag all taped to hell and yonder and felt like stone the first time you tagged it. Brother thank God for the priests and nuns at the orphanage, don't you ever forget them, roger that, all the love they gave you, all they taught you about life. No way you could have made it without them, no way in hell. And buddy, Tommy is just a kid. Seems like a million years ago when you were his age. Don't you ever forget he's just a kid, Jesse thought now, just a kid whose whole world fell apart in a heartbeat. Don't you ever forget he's just a kid. Just a kid who's going through a world of hurt.

"All right, Jesse, but you've gotta' tell me *why* your hair is like Santa Claus. 'Cause you're not related to Santa Claus! You knew I was gonna' ask you that, you're just like my granddad, he can tell what I'm gonna' say! But I gotta' tell you something, you look older than my granddad! And my granddad is seventy years old this year, he turned seventy in October but you look *older* than him. I mean, at least your hair does, you look like an old man! Why do you look so old, Jesse?"

Jesse laughed, looking at him. He was shaking his head and grinning and laughing, looking at Tommy in the snow.

"My hair turned all gray when I was thirty, buddy. Strangest thing, just one of those things nobody can really explain. Life is full of surprises and some of them are pleasant but that surprise was not so pleasant, no indeed. Strangest damn thing. But what are you gonna' do, eh? Premature gray, the folks with stethoscopes call it. Went all silver when I was thirty-eight, that was five years ago."

Tommy shook his head, frowning, looking up at him.

"The folks with the *what*?," Tommy said, scratching his head. "Who are they, Jesse? Who are the folks with the what, what did you call it, the stethowhichamacallit?"

Jesse grinned, looking at him.

"Doctors, buddy. Doctors. Carry. Stethoscopes. Doctors carry stethoscopes around their necks — "

" — And it feels cold, Jesse, when they put the metal thing against my chest. The stethowhichamacallits have the black rubber tube things that go around the doctors' necks."

"Stethoscopes, buddy."

"Right. Stethoscopes!"

"That's right," Jesse said, laughing. "Roger that on the stethoscopes. Let's chop some wood, Tommy."

Tommy kicked at some pine needles on the ground and looked over at his mother and father standing on the porch of the mountain cabin and they waved to him and went inside the cabin.

Looking back at Jesse now, Tommy frowned, folding his arms across his chest. Shaking his head, Tommy gestured toward the axes leaning up against the oak tree.

"But my dad and mom told me that you'd teach me how to box, Jesse! I want to hit the heavy bag like a real boxer! My dad and mom told me last night that this would be a lot of fun and I'd hit the big heavy bag and I'd learn how to box. They told me you were a Ranger and you stood for our people before I was born, you and Father James were both Rangers together and you defended our country, you were a real commando and everything. And Father James was a real commando and you met each other in the Rangers. You were commandos, together! Before I was born! But they didn't say anything about chopping wood. They told me I'd hit the heavy bag like a real boxer. What does chopping wood have to do with boxing? I chop wood at home. And lumberjacks chop wood. Paul Bunyan chopped wood. But I don't wanna' be a lumberjack. I don't want to chop wood, I want to fight. I want to learn how to box, Jesse. I want to hit the heavy bag. My mom and dad told me that you'd teach me boxing. My mom and dad told me that I'd hit the heavy bag and it would be fun, hitting the heavy bag. There's two heavy bags hanging from the trees, I can see them. I wanna' hit the heavy bags! Why can't I put on some boxing gloves and hit the heavy bags?"

McCullough grinned now, looking at Tommy, and fished a photograph out of a pocket of his gray hooded sweat shirt.

"That's Jack Dempsey, Tommy," he said, taking a knee and handing the photograph to Tommy. "Heavyweight boxing champion from 1919 to 1926. Grew up north of here, in Montana.

He chopped wood every day, before he'd hit the heavy bag. You know where Montana is?"

Tommy nodded quickly to him and said, "I do, I know where Montana is, it's next to Canada and there's a lot of snow and grizzly bears in Montana. Canada is the land of the Great Far North and Montana is just below Canada. And Montana has real glaciers and big rivers and real bears! My dad told me that in Montana, there are grizzly bears and brown bears and mountain lions. My dad is half Navajo and my mom is all Navajo and my dad told me the Lakota tribe is up in Montana, and the Crow and Cheyenne, too. My mom told me to never feed a grizzly bear. I must never feed a grizzly bear! She said there are real grizzly bears in Montana. My mom told me to never feed black bears and brown bears, too, I guess I must never feed a bear anywhere, Jesse. Grizzly bears are very big but the polar bears are in Canada and they are like big white Godzilla bears. I must stay away from the Godzilla bears. There are no big white Godzilla bears in Montana, Jesse. But Montana has real grizzly bears!"

"That's right," Jesse said, laughing and standing up. "Don't ever try and feed a grizzly bear, buddy, or you'll end up as a meal for the grizzly, ain't life strange. Roger that on the big white Godzilla bears, too. Now, what's Jack Dempsey got in his hands, in that photo?"

Tommy stared at the photo of Jack Dempsey in his prime, his thick dark hair slicked back, wearing dark trousers and a gray crew neck sweatshirt, a white towel around his neck in a black and white photo taken of Dempsey chopping wood at his training camp in 1919, before he'd won the heavyweight crown from Jess Willard in that same year.

"An axe," Tommy said quickly. "Mr. Jack Dempsey has an axe in his hands, Jesse. Mr. Jack Dempsey looks tough, he looks like he could just look at somebody and make them not want to fight him, I'll bet nobody messed with him. He looks young, too, for a heavyweight champion. He sure looks young. You sure he was a heavyweight, Jesse? He doesn't look that big. He doesn't look big at all, he's not a big guy like my dad. My dad is six foot four. Mr. Jack Dempsey is kinda' skinny for a heavyweight, too. I mean, he's got mighty big shoulders but he doesn't look big enough to be a heavyweight. He's lean! Mrs. Scofield is my first grade teacher. Mrs. Scofield says that lean means the same as skinny. Mrs. Scofield says that if we eat our brussel sprouts and potatoes and steak and lemon meringue pie, we will not be skinny and we will grow up big and strong. But Mr. Jack Dempsey sure was lean. You sure he was heavyweight champion, Jesse?"

Jesse folded his arms, smiling, and chuckling under his breath.

"Tommy, the guy he beat to take the title was over six feet six inches tall and outweighed Jack Dempsey by over fifty pounds. That goliath of a man, Jess Willard, you'd probably call him a walking Godzilla. I'll tell you what, Jess Willard was not as big as a polar bear but he was a mighty big man and he had a right hand like a sledgehammer and it didn't matter."

"Then why did Jack Dempsey beat him, Jesse?," Tommy asked, frowning. "Why didn't it matter that Mr. Jess Willard was a big Godzilla man and Mr. Jess Willard had a right hand like a sledgehammer?"

"Because Jack Dempsey had a left hook like God," Jesse said slowly, looking the boy in his eyes. "Truth be told, Tommy, Dempsey had thunder in both hands. Like Marciano. Rocky Marciano was another heavyweight champ, Jesse, and he knocked out guys with one punch, either hand. He was a real two-fisted brawler, Marciano. Now, Jack Dempsey dropped heavyweights with overhand rights, right hooks, right uppercuts, left hooks, left uppercuts and straight lefts. Truth, Dempsey was mean like a street fighter, too, 'cause he'd *been* a street fighter. He walked into a boxing ring, well, he came to fight. Dempsey was fierce. Tommy,

Jack Dempsey used to walk into saloons out West when he was just a kid and challenge miners and gamblers, fully-grown men, to fight him. That's when he was fourteen years old and about one hundred and forty five pounds, soaking wet. If he'd lost those fights, he would not have eaten. He had to fight to put food on the table, literally. And nobody went to the body like Dempsey, he broke ribs, he could really bust a guy up inside. He was something else. Marciano was like Dempsey in some ways, too, but he wasn't on fire right from the sound of the first bell, right in the first round, like Dempsey was. See those stones on the ground near that pit, buddy?"

Tommy nodded quickly, glancing at the stones on top of the green tarp.

"Well, that's where Marciano got his upper-cuts from, standing in a pit like that and squatting down and picking up a stone and throwing it up like this," Jesse said, and he walked over to the pit and Tommy followed him and Jesse leapt down into the pit and said, "Now, climb the ladder down in here and toss a couple stones, just like me."

Grabbing a stone that weighed about sixty pounds, Jesse squatted down in the pit now and tossed it left to right across his body, his left hand following through like he was throwing a left up-percut as he tossed the stone up on the canvas now. Tommy watched the stone fall and thump on the canvas and he climbed down the ladder into the pit.

"Take this one, Tommy," he said to the boy now and Tommy grabbed the small stone Jesse pointed out to him, the stone weighing roughly fifteen pounds. Tommy tossed the stone from left to right, across his body, heaving it up out of the pit. Jesse nodded to him, squinting.

Tommy grabbed another stone of about the same size and tossed it in the same way and Jesse said to him, grinning, "Not easy, is it, buddy?"

"No, these stones are heavy, Jesse! This is like real Spartacus stuff, I never did anything like this before! I saw that Spartacus stuff on *youtube*, the gladiators are on *youtube* and Spartacus, he was a gladiator and then he stopped being a gladiator and he got free. This is real Spartacus stuff, Jesse. Mr. Marciano did this to train for boxing? Mr. Marciano did the Spartacus stuff? Did he chop wood, too? He must have been tough."

Jesse nodded to him, smiling, and said, "He sure did chop wood. Marciano *had* to be tough, Tommy, he was about 5'11" and 185 pounds and he was fighting guys well over 200 pounds and much taller than him, guys who were six two, six three. He knocked out a guy who was 240 pounds. Nobody trained like Marciano, buddy. Marciano ate pushups for breakfast and heavy bags for lunch. And like Dempsey, Marciano could knock a guy out cold with either hand. I'll tell you what, let's get out of the pit. I usually save the pit until after chopping wood. Let's go," gesturing toward the ladder.

Climbing the ladder out of the pit, Tommy said, "Jesse, how tall was Jack Dempsey?"

"Six one. And he weighed less than 200 pounds."

"So he was kind of small, for a heavyweight," Tommy said, walking through the trees in the snow on the mountain now and nodding to him. "But he really was the champion?"

Jesse nodded back, smiling and saying, "Yes, he *really* was the champ, buddy. Absolutely. Now, Dempsey was smaller than a lot of heavyweights but it didn't matter, buddy. Jack Dempsey had power and speed and guts. He'd fight you in the middle of a river if he had to, he'd fight in the middle of the Mojave Desert if he had to, he was a fighter through and through. Tommy, before Dempsey was champ, long before he was champ, well, he had to get from one town to another, to line up his fights, so he could fight and make enough money to eat."

"Did he drive a car, to get from one town to another, Jesse?," Tommy asked, shoving his hands in his trouser pockets.

Jesse smiled, saying, "No indeed, Tommy, no. He was poor, way too poor to own a car. No, he rode the trains for free."

"He rode the trains for free? How did he ride a train without buying a *ticket*?," Tommy asked, shaking his head, his eyes giving new definition to quizzical.

"He rode underneath the train, Tommy. He held on to the steel rods on the undercarriage of a train car. That's how."

"But if he'd fallen off, he would've died," Tommy said, his eyes wide. "The train would've crushed him, he would've *died!*"

"Falling off was not in his plan, though, was it?"

"No. No, it sure wasn't in his plan," Tommy said now, shaking his head slowly. "Mr. Jack Dempsey. He made sure he didn't fall off, Jesse, he sure made sure of that. He just hung on to the bottom of those trains, like a bird on a wire but upside down. Wow. He had to hang on and never give up."

Jesse nodded to the boy.

"Damn straight, Tommy. He had to hang on and never give up. That's why his wrists got so big and that's why his hands were so strong. Jack Dempsey could break a man's hand, just shaking hands, I kid you not."

"He held on, underneath the train!," Tommy

exclaimed, his eyes still wide, "Whoa, whoa, that's beast! That's beast! 'Cause, 'cause, Jesse he did that 'cause he wanted to save money, is that right, 'cause he was so poor?"

Jesse nodded to him.

"It's tough being poor, buddy, and Jack Dempsey damned sure didn't want to stay poor. Best way to help the poor is not to become one of them. Nobody who's ever been poor wanted to stay poor. I'll tell you something I know from my own life: I've been poor and I've been rich and rich is better. Dempsey knew all about that, too. And you're absolutely right, buddy, to save money, Dempsey rode from town to town underneath a train, just holding on. That's how he got from one place to another, Tommy. If he'd ever let go, he would have died, like you said, his body would have been all mangled up by those trains and the railway tracks. And Tommy, let me tell you straight up, no joke, let me tell you something: Jack Dempsey had *heart*. There's a saying in boxing: You can't train heart. Tommy, you can't train courage. Can't teach it. When you're fighting for a meal and a roof over your head from day to day, like Dempsey was in his teens, just eight years older than you are now when he first started fighting to put bread on the table, well, you've gotta' be brave just to survive. Think about that, buddy.

Just eight years older than you are right now. He'd walk into a saloon in a mining camp and say, "I can whip any man here."

"He'd fight those men in those saloons?"

Jesse nodded to him.

"That's right. Dempsey was just a teenager but he was damn sure already a man. And he was fighting for his breakfast, lunch and supper. Remember I told you that he weighed about 145 pounds, Tommy, when he was just fourteen?"

Tommy nodded quickly to him, saying "Yessir."

"Well, that's welterweight, Tommy, 145 pounds. Jack Dempsey was fighting men who were natural light heavyweights and natural heavyweights. *Men.* Full-grown men who had worked outdoors all their lives, men who were lumberjacks and miners and combat veterans."

"That made the men angry, Jesse, didn't it," Tommy said, his eyes hard now, his eyebrows raised. "Jack Dempsey was smart, he knew they'd fight him if he told those grown men that he could whip them. 'Cause he was just a kid and he looked skinny as a scarecrow but they were real men, like my dad is a real man and like my granddad is a real man and like you're a real man. My mom told me that I will be a real man too, when I grow up," and he looked at Jesse now like he was looking at a friend.

"I'm sure you will be, buddy," Jesse said to him, nodding to Tommy and smiling and reaching out a hand.

"And my dad told me that the best thing about a real man is that he has a good heart," Tommy said, shaking hands, "he told me that a real man does not disrespect other people, it doesn't matter how tough a man is if he doesn't have a good heart. A real man does not disrespect people. That's what my dad told me! My dad told me that I must never disrespect another man and I must never disrespect women, I must give a pretty girl flowers on Easter. My mom told me that's true, too, when I asked her, she said that the most important thing about a real man is that he has a good heart, that's what makes him a real man. And I told my mom what my dad said, that I must give a pretty girl flowers on Easter and my mom laughed and said that's true and I asked her if she was joking 'cause she laughed, you know, and my mom told me no, it's true, my dad told me the truth."

Jesse nodded and winked at him, smiling.

"Buddy, your mom and dad are right, it's always good to give a pretty girl flowers on Easter. Always give a pretty girl a kiss and never break her heart. Your mom and dad told you straight, roger that."

"Jesse, what does *roger that* mean? You said that

a couple times. I never heard that before. Where'd you learn that?," Tommy said quickly, clapping his hands.

"Means *yes*, buddy. Means yes in a very good way. Means *yes, absolutely*. I learned that phrase in the Rangers, Tommy."

"So that's commando language. US Army Rangers say it, they say, "*Roger that.*" That's what commandos say," Tommy said. "I'm gonna' tell my friends at school that I learned commando language from Mr. Jesse McCullough. I can speak commando language, now! I'm gonna' teach my friends to say, *Roger that.*"

Jesse grinned and replied, "Yes indeed, that's commando language. Roger that. Good to see you've got your thinking cap on, champ. Now you're right—"

"—Roger that," Tommy said, grinning. "And I'm gonna' tell my friends about Mr. Jack Dempsey, he hung on to the bottom of those trains. He was tough! He held on to the steel rods and he rode for free and he was poor but he didn't stay poor and he never gave up and he was smart, he was real smart, he won those fights in the mining camps and saloons so he could survive. He fought those men who were real men and he beat them and he was just a teenager, he was just eight years older than I am right now! And he lived out West, like

us. That's how it was out West, back in the olden days, wasn't it?"

Jesse nodded, looking the boy in his eyes.

"Roger that, buddy, Dempsey was mighty smart and mighty clever and he was damn sure tough. He had to be tough, you're right, that's how it was out West, it was rough in a lot of places. Some men had to fight to survive and Dempsey was one of them. See, you're a grown man, a real man like you said, handling a pick and a shovel all day inside a silver mine in the mountains in Montana, for instance. You're forty years old and it's 1910 and when you were, say, fifteen in 1885, you started out as a lumberjack in Oregon or Idaho or Montana, no chainsaws back then, just axes and saws, serious work. Now, a fair share of those miners in 1910 had fought in the Spanish-American War, or in China or Haiti or the Philippines in the Army or Marines. So, you're a miner and a combat veteran and you've survived some hard times in your life. And now a youngster, like you said, Tommy, looking like a scarecrow because he's so damn skinny, not even fifteen years old, well he looks at you with a smart-aleck grin and tells you that he can whip you. Hard to walk away from that, Tommy, especially if there's money on the table. And everyone in the bar, betting on the fight, you know for a fact that they are going to bet on the miner, not on the kid. So that's a lot of money riding on that fella' who's gonna' fight yonder Jack Dempsey, that's a lot of money bet against Dempsey. Only they didn't know what the world was soon to discover about Jack Dempsey, they didn't know that he could drop a man standing six foot six and 240 pounds with one punch, left hand or right hand, drop him and stop him. They didn't know that Dempsey had a left hook like God and a right hand like a runaway train. And even if you'd told those folks betting big money against Dempsey that Dempsey had that kind of power, they'd never believe you, because a guy who's 145 pounds, soaking wet, is never, ever supposed to be able to knock out a man as big as a heavyweight fighter. You're absolutely right, Dempsey was smart. The smartest thing about him is that he believed in himself. You've got to believe in yourself to survive in this world. Now, if Jack Dempsey had lost those street fights and bar brawls and pick-up fights in mining camps in Montana, he would have starved, he would not have survived. He never would have made it. He had to fight to survive. I tell you what, Tommy, I think that if Jack Dempsey had not made it as a boxer, he would have ended up in jail or a graveyard before his twentieth birthday. And you're right, he has an axe in his hands in this photo. Well-honed axe, too, mighty sharp axe, given the reflection off the edge of that axe blade. There are no shadows spreading out on the ground near the trees in this photo, so it was taken in the middle of the day, likely at high noon. Can you see the heavy bags behind him, hanging off that steel pole?"

Tommy leaned in, looking closely at the photo. "Yes."

"Can you see the rope of the boxing ring, on the edge of the photo, buddy?"

Tommy nodded, looking up at him now.

"And of course, that's an axe in his hand, in this photo."

"Yessir, Jesse, that's a mighty big axe, too."

"You know why he's carrying an axe in this photo, Tommy?"

"No," Tommy said, shrugging.

"Because there's no better way to start training for boxing than chopping wood. Now let me hear you say that."

Tommy looked at him.

"Say what, Jesse?"

Jesse grinned, looking at him.

"Just say this, just like me: There's no better way to start training for boxing than chopping wood."

"There's no better way to start training for boxing than chopping wood," Tommy said, a fierce look in his eyes now. "There's no better way to start training for boxing than chopping wood! Chopping wood! Chopping wood! Chop, chop, chop! I'm gonna' chop wood just like Jack Dempsey, yeah! Jack Dempsey chopped wood and then he hit the heavy bags, chop, chop, chop!"

"Most excellent, champ," Jesse said, smiling. "Do you know how to chop wood?"

Tommy nodded quickly, looking at him.

"Yessir. My dad taught me last year. I can chop wood and I can split wood and I can stack wood. I know how to use a tomahawk, too. Did you ever carry a tomahawk when you were a commando, when you were in the Rangers? Did you and Father James carry tomahawks? My dad told me that Father James was a commando and then he became a man of God and now, Father James is our priest and he wears black all the time and he gets free cups of coffee wherever he goes and my dad and mom call him Padre. Becky is Father James' wife and she makes the best chocolate chip cookies ever! My mom likes to say, "Becky is a kind lady." And me and my Dad chop wood for Father James and Becky and they always thank us and Becky tells us after we unload the wood from my dad's vehicle, "Now come on in and have some hot chocolate and cookies." That's mighty kind of Becky. And Becky teases Father James and she tells Father James that the real reason he became a priest is because he gets free cups of coffee. Becky is funny! O no don't tell my mom I said that, Jesse! OK? Don't tell my mom that I said Becky makes the best chocolate chip cookies ever."

"What's said on the mountain stays on the mountain, chief," Jesse said, reaching out a hand to him. "No worries, that will be our secret. Becky is a great lady, you know that Father James met her in New Mexico, when he was a hunting guide."

"I didn't know that, Jesse. Does that mean she is a New Mexican lady?"

Jesse nodded, saying, "That's right, buddy."

"And Father James was a hunting guide, too? Before he wore the black robe, he was a hunting guide? That's what my granddad says about Father James, he says, "Father James wears the black robe." Father James wears the black robe, Jesse. But he didn't always wear the black robe, I guess. And he was a commando *and* a hunting guide?"

Jesse nodded to him, watching birds over mountains far in the distance.

"He was, indeed. After he got out of the Rangers, Father James was a hunting guide, here and in New Mexico and Namibia — Namibia is in southwest Africa, Tommy. Father James was a hunting guide for thirteen years, before he became a padre, buddy."

"What does Padre mean, Jesse?"

"Means father in Spanish. We use it in Spanish, also, to mean a Catholic priest, buddy. We use padre in English, too, to mean a man of God. There's a lot of Spanish words that came into English and that's one of them, Tommy," Jesse said, handing him an axe. "Now, did Father James and I carry tomahawks in the Rangers? Knives and machetes, yes, but tomahawks, well, I hate to disappoint you but we never carried any tomahawks back in the day. Your dad told you right about Father James, I certainly remember when he wasn't wearing a black suit to work."

"Father James wears all black at Mass," Tommy said, matter-of-factly. "But when he's with Becky, he likes to wear cowboy boots and blue jeans and a black leather jacket. I thought Father James was related to another James, too, but my Dad told me that he's not related to the other James, but he's kind of related to the other James, I mean, he's sort of related to the other James and that's OK. I guess Father James is kind of like a cousin, to the other James."

"Who is the other James that you thought Father James was related to, champ?," Jesse asked, folding his arms, looking Tommy in his eyes.

"James Taylor, Jesse! 'Cause Father James listens to James Taylor's songs so much and so I asked my dad if Father James and James Taylor are brothers and my dad told me, "Sort of, more like cousins," and me and my dad listen a lot to this song that James Taylor sings, "Fire and Rain." I didn't know who was singing that song, "Fire and Rain," the first time I heard it and I remember I was four years old and we were coming back from the county fair and I heard it and I liked that song very much. So I asked my dad who sang it and he told me, "James Taylor," and I said that his name was just like Father James and my dad said, "That's right." My dad says that it is a great song and Father James told me that it is a great song, too, and my mom told me that she loves that song and that it is a great song too and when I listen to it, I feel better. And you know what?"

Jesse smiled, looking at him.

"What, buddy?"

"Becky listens to James Taylor's songs, too, and Becky and Father James listen to this lady sing, too, my dad and mom told me the lady is named Carole King! And James Taylor sings another song, *The Water is Wide* and Carole King sings *It's Too Late* and *So Far Away*, those are good songs too, Jesse. I like them. I like those songs. My dad says Father James is cool and my mom says Father James is a good man and my dad and mom drink coffee with

Father James and Becky and listen to the songs by James Taylor and Carole King. Do you listen to the songs by James Taylor and Carole King, Jesse? Do you have a black leather jacket, too? My dad doesn't have a black leather jacket. My dad has a brown leather jacket and my mom tells him to take out the trash."

Jesse laughed, grinning.

"I'll bet she does, yes indeed. I sure do listen to James Taylor and Carole King, buddy. For a long time, now, since I was your age, as a matter of fact. No, I don't have a black leather jacket, Tommy, sorry about that. I've got a brown leather jacket, though, up at the cabin. Now, with any luck, we might get around to your tomahawk. But that axe you've got, that axe will have to do today. Tell me something. Can you throw a tomahawk, champ?"

Tommy shook his head, axe in his hand.

"Not yet. My dad told me last summer that I could learn how to throw it, if I want to. He was going to teach me and Billy. And Billy died," Tommy said, not smiling now and looking at Jesse like he was looking into the eye of a hurricane.

Jesse could see a sadness in his eyes now like he'd never seen before in anyone in his life. The wind blew cold on them from out of the west, dusting their boots with snow.

May God's love be with you, Jesse thought

now, looking at Tommy and praying a Hail Mary in his heart for the boy.

"Billy died on the playground at school," Tommy said, speaking slowly, his eyes grim and his voice low, looking in Jesse's eyes now. "We just stood there, Jesse. We just stood there and watched him die. None of us knew what to do. I didn't know what to do. I just stood there and watched him die. He was right next to me, Billy was right next to me when he died. He couldn't say anything. His eyes were awful and it all happened so fast. He was dead just like that and we cried, we cried, we cried. We cried and screamed, it was all so fast. The doctor said there was nothing we could have done. Blood came out of Billy's mouth. He just dropped dead right next to me. The doctor told us a blood vessel blew up in Billy's brain. Billy was my best friend, Jesse. We learned how to chop wood together and we used to walk to school every day and we played football together. We were on the same team. Billy was a wide receiver, he could run real fast. My dad said that Billy ran like the wind. It was fun, playing football with him. You knew he could always score the touchdown. We used to play checkers at recess, too. He liked this girl in our class, her name is Alice. She's a nice girl and she always wins the spelling bees and she's full-blooded Navajo, like my mom. Billy never told Alice that he liked her but she used to smile at him and he gave her some flowers, the day after Halloween. I think she knew that Billy liked her. Alice came to the funeral and she cried. She cried as much as Billy's mom. My mom and dad hugged Alice after the funeral and talked to her parents, and Billy's parents talked to her, too, and they hugged her and dried her face with the bandanas like the cowboys wear. Me and Billy learned how to ride horses last year and we wore the bandanas around our necks, like the cowboys. Billy was a full-blooded Navajo and he was my best friend but he's all gone now."

Jesse took a knee. Tommy looked at him and the boy was crying, looking at Jesse and wiping his tears away. The sun was bright on them, shadows from the pines on the mountain falling on them in the snow. Jesse pulled a faded olive green bandana out of his sweatshirt.

"I'm very sorry about your buddy, Tommy, I'm very sorry that Billy died," Jesse said softly, handing him the bandana now. He dried his face with the bandana and began to hand it back to Jesse.

"No, you keep it, I've got plenty of those. Tommy, do you see the leather hanging from the porch yonder?," Jesse asked him now, standing up and gesturing toward the cabin.

Picking up an axe, Jesse slammed it into a log as Tommy nodded to him.

"There's stuff on all those pieces of leather, Jesse," Tommy said, wiping tears from his face, "feathers and beads and stuff. And some kind of metal, I think, on each one. Why are they there? They look like triangles. Did you put them there, Jesse?"

Jesse nodded.

"Why?," Tommy asked, squinting. "What do they mean?"

"Take a seat on that log," Jesse said to him now, gesturing toward the log he'd slammed his axe into as ravens swooped through the pines, flying south toward Chinle.

The boy sat down on the log and Jesse kicked a big chunk of pine toward him and sat down on it, opposite the boy.

"They're all prayer flags, Tommy. Every one of those pieces of leather is a prayer flag for someone who died with me at war," Jesse said, looking in his eyes. "They died right next to me, too, just like Billy died right next to you. I've lost some good friends, too. They're all gone, too. They had people who loved them, just like Billy's family loved him. They had good friends and they had best friends. Just like Billy was your best friend. Each one of those prayer flags has something they cherished on it—leather from one of their packs, bits of glass and metal from a compass they carried, cloth from the clothes they wore when they died. When you wake up in the morning, you can still see Billy's face, can't you?"

Tommy nodded to him and his eyes were wide now.

"And I'll bet you're wondering how I knew that, aren't you?"

Tommy nodded quickly, squinting.

"I knew that because I still see the faces of all the men I went to war with who never came back to America, Tommy. And other men from other countries, British and Australian men, French and Kurdish and Malaysian. Comrades. Good friends. They never came back to their homes, either, Tommy. I was the last face they saw on this earth. They were my good friends, my best friends. I trusted them with my life and they trusted me with their lives. They were the best men I've ever known, they were men like Father James, and they died right next to me at war. But that's not as tough, I think, as what you're going through. That's not as tough as Billy dying right next to you on that playground at school."

Tommy gazed at him, a thoughtful look come over him now, looking Jesse in his eyes.

"Why not, Jesse? Why not? They were your best friends, like Billy was my best friend. And I see Billy's face when I wake up in the morning, just like you see your best friends' faces when you wake up in the morning. It's hard, isn't it Jesse?"

Jesse nodded to him, looking in his eyes.

"Yes it is, Tommy."

Tommy nodded to him, biting his lower lip now and breathing out slowly.

"Maybe it's just as hard for you as it is for me, Jesse. Maybe it is harder for me, like you say. I'm sorry about your friends, Jesse. I'm sorry they died. You were right there next to them when they died. Like Billy. Billy was right next to me and then he just died. He just died. I wish Billy had never died. He just fell down and died. We were playing on the jungle gym at school. He was climbing the monkey bars and he just fell off. He just died right there next to me. I thought he was just fooling around, you know. Billy was real funny, he liked to play tricks on us, he was always fooling around like that. And he just laid there and Mrs. Scofield ran over to us and she screamed. She screamed so loud. Mrs. Scofield is a serious teacher but she is kind to us and she tells us to be good and we must not tell a lie and she tells us to do our homework. My dad and mom told me that Mrs. Scofield has a good heart and that I must respect her and I do. Mrs. Scofield saw Billy in the dirt with the blood coming out of his mouth and she screamed. Sometimes, like when it's that time of day and I'm on the playground and I look at the monkey bars, I can still hear her screaming. I can still hear Mrs. Scofield screaming, Jesse. God took Billy away, Jesse. That's mean. That's real mean. God is mean. That's mean, for God to take Billy away. Billy was my best friend and now he's dead and nothing makes sense. I keep seeing these psychologists. You're not like them. I'm sorry about your friends, Jesse. I'm sorry that they died, too."

Tommy laid his axe down and reached his arms out and Jesse hugged him, patting him on his back.

"That's mighty kind of you, buddy," Jesse said, wiping tears from his eyes. "That's mighty kind."

Standing up now, Jesse folded his arms, speaking softly to the boy.

"I think that losing a best friend like Billy is harder for you, Tommy, harder than me being at war and seeing my best friends die, because in this life, especially at your age, you never expect to see a good friend like Billy, heck, anyone, drop dead right next to you. Everywhere that I've been at war, I knew that I could lose my life and I knew that my friends might die, too. That didn't make it any easier when they were killed in action, but that's a helluva' lot less difficult to deal with than seeing your best friend die right next to you on a playground, Tommy.

Nothing I went through as a kid was as tough as what you're going through. Billy was just a first-grader, just like you, right?"

Tommy nodded quickly, his eyes bright.

"That's right," he said softly to Jesse now, his lips pursed. "Billy was in the first grade with me. We were in the same class, Mrs. Scofield's class. She cried the next day, too. And she cried at Billy's funeral and her husband cried, too. There sure are a lot of tears in this world. I wish God could stop all the tears in this world, Jesse. Where is God, Jesse? You know what, me and Billy went to kindergarten together, too. And we used to go hunting for arrowheads and the tips of spears, my mom always told us to be careful picking up the arrowheads and spear tips 'cause they're still sharp. But we never cut our hands, we always carried old leather scraps that my dad gave us and we'd wrap up the arrowheads and spear tips in the old leather. It was fun, Billy said that every time we picked up an arrowhead, that meant we would get good luck from the spirits of the Navajo who'd made that arrowhead and who'd shot that arrow. Billy was full-blooded Navajo, not like me, the kids tease me all the time at school 'cause I'm not a full-blooded — "

Jesse gestured to him and Tommy got quiet now.

"You're a full-blooded American, buddy," Jesse said, his eyes hard, speaking slowly to the boy now. "You be proud to be from Arizona, Tommy, and you be proud to be an American. You've got a lot of Navajo in you and the Navajo are a great people, a great tribe. The Navajo fought like lions for America in World War Two and our country owes the Navajo a tremendous debt. And your dad loves you and your mom loves you and you've got a long life ahead of you, God willing. You see that hawk flying over yonder, alone, over those pines and that snow north of us, over those mountains north of us?"

Tommy nodded, looking at the hawk in the sky.

"God's in that hawk, Tommy. God's in that hawk and God is in that wind and God is with us now and forever and always, here on this mountain with you and wherever you may roam, always. You asked where God is, well, I lived with folks on the other side of the Pacific, people of the mountains just like the Navajo are people of these mountains. Pawkinyaun tribe of Northern Thailand, that's in Asia, Tommy. They have a saying: *A hawk flies high and never alone.* They see the spirit of God in the hawks in the sky and the wind on a river and the bright gold of sunshine and the beauty of stars in the night. God's in that hawk and the wind that's carrying the hawk over those pines and that snow. God was with me when I lost Jack Thurgood and David Storm on a mission at war, seems like just yesterday," Jesse said as Tommy wiped tears from his eyes. "Nothing makes sense sometimes, buddy. Nothing comes at you harder than life. Nothing slams into you and breaks your heart harder than life, Tommy. You lost a good friend and I know it's hard, harder than anything I've been through at war. Harder than anything I've been through at war because when you go to war, you know you might die and you know that the men you go to war with might die. You know that, going in. You know that you're not going to come back home with every one you went to war with. And it still hurts, when I wake up in the morning and see their faces, the faces of my comrades who never made it back and the faces of people whose lives we tried to save but couldn't. Still hurts. Like it hurts for you but I want you to know something. Once you accept that hurt — and that's a very hard thing, Tommy — but once you realize that the hurt is always going to be with you, you'll find a peaceful feeling in you and you can deal with the hurt and carry on and live life with a whole heart, with a strong heart, with a happy heart and with joy for every sunrise, with joy for every sunset, with joy for every day and every night. Only *you* can help *you* find that peaceful feeling. Only you can decide to accept that pain and carry on. But here's the juice: You've got no choice *but* to accept that pain and carry on. Because if you don't accept that pain and realize that it's never really, truly going to go away, then it *will* destroy you like it's been destroying you. And I know that's gotta' be very, very hard for you to understand, my God you are only six years old. I know that must be a very difficult thing to understand, Tommy. I know how hard it must feel for you because I know how hard it felt for me, when I was an orphan, here in Northern Arizona, growing up without a mother and father to help me understand life. Growing up without a mother and father to talk to, to laugh with, to sit around a fireplace with, to have breakfast with, to ask questions to — growing up without a mother and father to read stories to me at night. Growing up without a mother and father to talk to about life, growing up without a mother and father to talk to about God. Life for me, when I was your age, buddy, life was just pain every day. Nothing but pain. When I was four and five and six, heck, when I was two and three, for that matter, I cried myself to sleep every night. Every night, buddy. I kid you not. Every night I cried myself to sleep. Until I learned how to box and that helped a lot, learning how to hit the heavy bag and feeling that pain go away a little with every punch I threw. But it wasn't until I accepted that pain as a part of me, as pain that was simply a part of my life, that I began to really live. That heavy bag became my father, it taught me to be strong and to believe in myself and to carry on. That heavy bag taught me to learn how to accept pain and never to feel sorry for myself. You must never feel sorry for yourself, Tommy. And pain is as much a part of life as joy. There's joy in our lives like there is sunshine in our lives and there's pain in our lives like there is rain in our lives. To get to the sunshine, you've gotta' make it through the rain. To get to the joy in life, you've gotta' hang tough and make it through the pain. That heavy bag was my father, buddy, it taught me to hang tough and to never say die. That heavy bag taught me to believe in myself. That heavy bag taught me to embrace the pain, to accept the pain and that heavy bag taught me to fight back. And then I really began to live, I mean live and enjoy being alive. I prayed real hard, Tommy, and I helped myself when I was your age right here in Northern Arizona, buddy. I prayed to God every night and I tried to make friends with everyone I met, because a priest told me when I was your age that life is better with every new friend you make, and when you make new friends, they become old friends, in time. And you keep your old friends and make new ones and life gets better because the more friends you have, the better life is. The priests and nuns at the orphanage helped me, too, they listened to me and they prayed with me and they taught me that love is real, because they loved me, like they loved all the kids at the orphanage. I didn't blame God or hate God for being an orphan, Tommy, it's not God's fault that my mother had such a hard life. I realized that I couldn't blame God for the choices that she made, the choices my mother made, they were all bad choices but they were her choices and at the end of the day, she gave me this life, she brought me into this world. Look, I'm gonna' tell you something that you may already know but I'm gonna' tell it to you anyways. Only *you* can help you. Only you can help you, Tommy. God helps those who help themselves, but only you can take that first step to help yourself, no one else can do that for you. And once you take that first step to help yourself, you'll feel a damn sight better and you'll take another step and you'll feel even better and you will find a peace in your heart and soul and spirit that you don't have now. And you can do that, you can do that for yourself just like I did that for myself thirty-seven years ago, when I was six years old just like you and just like you, I was right here, buddy, right here in Northern Arizona, hurting every day, hurting every day like you're hurting every day. There's a part of you that's always going to hurt and feel lonely and miss Billy, Tommy. That's the part of you that you have to accept now. Once you accept that hurt, you accept that pain, you'll find that pain is no longer dragging you down every day. Life changed you like life changed me. Buddy, the Chinese say, "Fall down seven times, get up eight times." You've been hammered, Tommy, you got hit with a haymaker by life. And life is what you make it. You can't let grief control your life. And you can't let grief control your future, buddy. You can't let that sadness dominate your life. You've got a great father and a great mother and they love you very much. I never had a mother and father, Tommy. And it was damn sad for me when I was your age until I accepted that pain and stopped feeling sorry for myself. I didn't let that grief dominate my life, and you can't let grief dominate your life, either."

Tommy looked hard at him.

"You didn't have a mom and dad, Jesse?"

Jesse nodded to him, his eyes calm and steady as he looked at the boy.

"Really?," he said softly to Jesse and Tommy was thinking now how it must be so very lonely, not having a mother and father, so lonely all the time how does somebody live without a mother and father, how did Jesse live without a mother and father. Jesse never had a mother to give a gift to on Mother's Day and he never had a father to give a gift to on Father's Day, Tommy thought now. He never had a mother to draw a happy face on his schoolwork like my mom draws a happy face on my schoolwork and he never had a dad to teach him how to chop wood and how to throw a football. He was just a little boy and he was all alone, just all alone.

"You were all alone when you were just a little boy, when you were a first-grader like me? You were all *alone*, really? Didn't you hate your mom and dad for leaving you all alone? Didn't you hate them, Jesse?"

Jesse looked Tommy in his eyes and Jesse was thinking that he'd never returned to Arizona since he'd volunteered for the Rangers and now I'm back on the side of a mountain right back here in Northern Arizona, a few mountains east of where I grew up, he thought now, mercy, trying to help a kid deal with his pain the way I dealt with my pain. Lord, give me strength. Twenty-four years since you set foot in Arizona. Swore you'd never return, well, reckon you'll never say never again, that's for damn sure. Twenty-four years. Never even changed planes in Phoenix, all this time, much less came back to these mountains. But you are here now and these blue skies are beautiful and it feels good to be alive, brother. Tommy is in the hurt locker like you were in the hurt locker when you were a kid. And you busted out of that hurt locker and never went back, you made it through the rain, by the grace of God and a heavy bag and the priests and nuns who loved you and taught you that love is real. Remember Father Ben at the orphanage in Flagstaff. Who told you that Joe Frazier had run in the snow in Philadelphia, training for The Night of the Left Hook. Remember when Father Ben had you running in the snow in Flagstaff and you were eight years old and man it hurt, that first time you were running in the snow with Father Ben up in the mountains north of Flagstaff, Father Ben sweating like a bear even in the cold and telling you, "Hang tough and carry on and believe in yourself, Jesse, look at Joe Frazier, he won that fight before he even stepped in the ring against Muhammad Ali. Joe Frazier won that fight when he was running in the snow in Philly, sweat turning to ice on his watch cap and wind damn cold in the winter in Philly and running in the snow, I'll tell you something about running in the snow, Jesse, it's like running in sand. Now Ali had never gone up against anyone like Joe Frazier, he'd never fought anyone who came at you like a street fighter and just kept coming on. And Ali couldn't block a left hook— God may forgive that but fighters don't. I taught you how to block a left hook yesterday for a reason, you've got to know how to block a left hook to have a chance at winning a fight. Buddy, Joe Frazier was a left hook machine that night, just left hook after left hook after left hook, all night long. Joe Frazier walked right through Ali's best punches and just kept coming on. Spirit of the warrior. Jesse, when you're running in the snow like Joe Frazier in Philly that winter, day in and day out, just taking the pain and hanging tough and never giving up, snow and ice and wind and never say die, never giving up on yourself and training like your life depends on it—well, there's just no way Joe Frazier could've lost that fight. Joe Frazier didn't go into that fight thinking about it like a fight, Jesse, Joe Frazier went into that fight like it was a war, he trained for that fight like a warrior trains for war. Night of the Left Hook, March 8th, 1971. And I want you to know something about Joe Frazier, Jesse, he defended kids from bullies when he was just a boy, not much older than you are now, Joe Frazier was just a kid then, just a kid growing up in South Carolina. Joe Frazier defended those kids, he defended his friends and stopped those bullies from hurting his friends. Jesse, it takes courage to stand up to bullies. Maybe you know that already but if you don't, it's good for you to know that now. You have to stand up to bullies in this world or they just bully more people, they just hurt more people. There's a word for Joe Frazier, Jesse, and that word is *brave*. He is a brave man and that's a good way to be in this world, Jesse, that's a good way to live. Look now, we made it back from the other side of the mountain, well-done, you can see Flagstaff now, hang tough, it's all downhill from here, go slow down this trail, there's ice in spots. Just follow me, follow the trail down through the pines. Looks like about two feet of snow, in a few places, go easy. You're doing good, Jesse, hang in there. Never say die, Jesse. Believe in yourself. You're running in the snow just like Joe Frazier, there's good karma in that, the Buddhists say. Can't say I disagree with them. Good karma is its own reward." Good karma, Jesse thought now, remembering Father Ben and Joe Frazier, good karma. Roger that. Father Ben. Tough and kind and fair. Man, he could tag a heavy bag. Hit the heavy bag for an hour every other day and taught you how to throw the double hook and double uppercut combination—left hook to the body, right hook to the head, bob and weave and right uppercut to the body, slide left and step inside and dig in and close it with a left uppercut to the head. Made you wear the weights on your wrists, punching the speed bag. Made you throw combinations with dumbbells in each hand—left jab, right cross, left hook to the body, right uppercut to the head, bob and weave, left hook to the head, right uppercut to the body, bob and weave, left uppercut to the body, slide right and step in and throw an overhand right. Father Ben, playing Sinatra's records on that old Kenwood turntable and he taught you how to sing *The Lady Is A Tramp* and Sister Cecilia got a kick out of that, God bless her. Sister Cecilia, who taught you how to pray the Rosary. Telling you to pray the Rosary every day and pray at the Shrine to Our Blessed Virgin Mary, Holy Mother of God. Bringing you and Father Ben hot cocoa and marshmallows when you'd come back from running in the snow. So kind. And Father Ben was cool, yes Lord. Dead five years now but he will never be forgotten. He understood respect and courage and honor and man, did he ever teach you well when he talked about Joe Frazier, mercy. Joe Frazier has gone on to higher ground, God rest his soul. A year and a half old, you were, when he rocked Ali in the 11th with the double left hook combination and dropped him in the 15th with a lead left hook. Father Ben told you that Ali never should have called Joe Frazier an Uncle Tom, taught you that lesson on respect, you have lived by that all your life. Told you that you should live like Joe Frazier, "Joe Frazier was class, Jesse, he was a man of respect and dignity and he never disrespected another fighter. Jesse, you must never disrespect anyone. What Ali did was just damn wrong, and shameful — as Shakespeare says in **Henry V**: *Shame, shame and nothing but shame.* And Joe Frazier taught Ali the meaning of respect, by the end of the 15th round in New York City." Amen to that. Joe Frazier, rest in peace, brother.

"Really, buddy," Jesse said now, his eyes cheerful and full of hope and his voice level and calm, looking Tommy in his eyes. "I never had a mother and father, growing up. So I never had brothers and sisters to play with, I never had a mother and father to talk to, to ask questions to, to listen to and to learn from and to love, I never had a mother and father to read me bedtime stories and to laugh with, to go hunting with and to have fun with, I never had cousins and uncles and aunts and grandparents. But I don't hate my mother, Tommy. I never knew my father so he's a ghost, and you can't love or hate a ghost, because you never know a ghost in the first place. Truth, my mother is a ghost to me, too, in many ways. All I know about my mother is that she was half-Apache and half-Irish and dirt-poor. And she left me at an orphanage in Flagstaff when I was five months old, no doubt because she realized that I'd be better off at the orphanage. That's love. That might be damned hard for you to understand, buddy, that may be impossible for you to understand but that's love. She loved me and she wanted me to have a better life than she could give me. That's love, Tommy — she thought about my situation, my condition, my life, ahead of her own life. That's love, buddy. She put my life above her own. And because she did that, she saved my life, in her way. No way I can hate her for that, or blame God for being an orphan. The world was throwing haymakers and left hooks and uppercuts at me, it felt like, when I was a kid — when I was your age, when I was six. But buddy, when the world is throwing punches at you, when the world is fighting you like it wants to break you, there's only one thing to do."

"What's that, Jesse?," Tommy said quickly, looking at him, the wind strong from out of the west now.

"Fight back. Don't let the world break you. Fight back, Tommy. Pray real hard and have a talk with God and believe in yourself, buddy. And don't be afraid to ask God to help you. He will help you, although it may not be exactly in the way you want Him to. Never say die. Never quit. Never give up. Fight back. Believe in yourself and never say die and keep fighting, as a buddy of mine in the Rangers liked to say, *Keep on keeping on*. There's a man I want you to learn from, to learn how to live with respect and dignity and to learn how to take the pain and carry on. That man is Joe Frazier, Tommy. When he was just a kid, buddy, just a couple years older than you are now, his friends were bullied by racists in South Carolina. His friends came to him for help. And he helped them, he held his own and defended his friends. He shut those bullies down, he stopped them from hurting his friends. Joe Frazier was a sharecropper's son and he made a difference in this world, he made life better for his friends. Don't ever let anyone tell you that you can't make a difference in this world, Tommy."

"That's how Billy was, Jesse, Billy hated bullies," Tommy said quickly, his eyes hard. "I like Mr. Joe Frazier, Jesse. Was he a fighter too, like Mr. Jack Dempsey and Mr. Marciano?"

"Joe Frazier was a heavyweight champion, Tommy, you're damn right he was a fighter," Jesse said, grinning and nodding to the boy now. "And he fought like a man on fire. He threw wicked left hooks and he ran in the snow in the winter of 1970, going into 1971. December 1970 and January 1971, he was running in the snow and training every day. He defended his friends from bullies and he never disrespected another fighter. Live with respect, Tommy. Live with respect and dignity, like Joe Frazier did. That's a good way to live, buddy."

Tommy nodded to him, a reflective look come over him.

"He ran in the snow, Jesse? That's *beast!*"

"I reckon that is beast," Jesse said, grinning.

"Jesse, I gotta' ask you a question. If you don't wanna' answer it, you don't have to."

Jesse nodded to him.

"Go ahead, buddy."

"Why did your mother leave you all alone? Didn't your father want to help you, even? Why didn't your father tell her, "No!" Why did she just up and leave you like that, Jesse?," Tommy said now, knocking the snow off his jacket.

Jesse smiled at him, a calm, peaceful look in his eyes.

"Tommy, there's things we can't explain in this world and my mother's situation is one of them—"

"—But don't you really hate her, Jesse, for what she did? I know you said you don't hate her but don't you *really* hate her, for leaving you all alone? Don't you really hate your father, too, I mean, why didn't your father help you?"

"You can't hate what you never had a chance to love, Tommy. You can't hate losing what you never had, in the first place. Tommy, I never knew my mother. I never had a chance to love her but I love what she did for me, when times were too hard for her to take care of me, when she knew that giving me up to the orphanage would save my life. And the truth is, given the hard times she was in, the truth is that the most loving thing she did for me was leaving me at the orphanage. No way I can hate my mother, Tommy, no way. And I'll tell you why: Because she loved me so much she found a way for me to survive in this world. So I don't hate her at all, Tommy, I just feel so damn sad for the life she was in, the life that destroyed her. She died so young and she had such a damn hard life, just a rough, rough life. I don't hate my mother, buddy, and that's the damn truth. That might be hard for you to understand but that's the truth. My mother was a prostitute and a heroin addict, Tommy. She was seventeen when she brought me into this world and she never saw her nineteenth birthday. Tommy, when my mother died, she was just twelve years older than you are right now. She was still a teenager when she died. There's no grave for her because she was cremated and her ashes were scattered over the desert south of Phoenix."

"So you can't take flowers to her grave," Tommy said, wiping tears from his eyes.

Jesse nodded to him and patted him on a shoulder.

"No, I can't, buddy. But every time I see a flower growing wild, I think that a part of my mother is in that flower, champ."

Tommy reached a hand out to him, looking in his eyes.

"I'm sorry about your mom, Jesse, I really am," the boy said softly. "It was the heroin that killed her, wasn't it? My dad and mom tell me all the time to stay away from drugs and Father James and Becky tell me that, too. And Mrs. Scofield tells us that too. Mrs. Scofield says, "Drugs kill. Don't let drugs kill you and stay away from people who use drugs, live a good life and don't do drugs. Don't get killed by drugs, don't do drugs." Mrs. Scofield has sad eyes when she tells us that. Mrs. Scofield's brother did not die from the heroin but he died from the crack cocaine, Jesse. I'm so sorry about your mom. I'm so sorry your mom died that way. And I'm sorry about Jack and David, I'm sorry about your friends who died at war. I guess you miss them, don't you?"

"That's mighty kind of you buddy," Jesse said, looking in his eyes. "And I do miss them, yes."

"Where were they from, Jesse?"

Jesse smiled at him.

"Jack Thurgood was from Northumberland, England, Tommy. And David Storm was from Melbourne, Australia. Good souls. And both of them very brave men."

Tommy nodded to him, squinting.

"Were they boxers, too?"

Jesse grinned, laughing.

"Well, no. But they both knew hand-to-hand combat very well. You're a little young to be learning hand-to-hand."

"Billy told me that's the Jason Bourne stuff! We watched it on *youtube*. Wow, they could do the Jason Bourne stuff! Can you do the Jason Bourne stuff too, Jesse?"

Jesse smiled at him and handed him the thermos of hot chocolate.

"Have some of that hot chocolate, buddy, I'm gonna' drink some coffee. And yes, I can do the Jason Bourne stuff, as you put it," chuckling, nodding to the boy.

"Thanks, Jesse," Tommy said, opening up the thermos and pouring the steaming hot chocolate into a plastic thermos cup and drinking it slowly as Jesse drank black coffee on the mountain with him.

"What were they like, Jesse," the boy said now, looking at him, a thoughtful, reflective look come over him now. "What were Jack and David like?"

Jesse gulped down his coffee and capped the black thermos. He could see a coyote on a ridgeline west of them, moving slowly in the snow under high blue skies in the mountains now.

"Jack was from the north of England," he said to the boy, "and he liked cigars, whiskey and women, in no particular order. He was a wild man and an excellent sniper. He had a girlfriend, a sweet woman named Sophia, in Milan, that's in Northern Italy, buddy. And David, well we always used to kid David that he should have been a history teacher. He had a degree in history and he loved the blues—blues music, buddy. He was a tracker, Tommy, and he was the best combat tracker I've ever seen. He was a great point man. He was a quiet man and he had a girlfriend in Singapore, Jenny."

Tommy capped his thermos now and handed it to Jesse, looking up in his eyes.

"They sure were good friends to you, weren't they, Jesse?," the boy said softly. Jesse nodded to him slowly and prayed a Hail Mary in his heart now, remembering his comrades.

"Yes they were, buddy. They were my best friends. They'd saved my life before and I'd saved their lives, a time or two. And they died trying to free people. In Burma, that's a long way from here."

"What was it like there?," Tommy asked, squinting.

"Jungles, thick jungles. And as many bad guys as there were trees," Jesse said, poker-faced. "Monsoon season, monsoon rain—that's night and day rain, walls of rain around the clock, we don't get rain like that up here. Mountains and jungle and monsoon rain. We were going up against the Burmese Army, who'd chained twenty farmers and their children. A lot of folks in chains, Tommy."

"You mean, like slaves? The bad guys had put the farmers and their little kids in chains, like slaves?"

Jesse nodded to him.

"And you freed the slaves?"

"With David on point and Jack up on a sniper rifle, yes," Jesse said softly, remembering that night in the rain and no moon and mist on a river. Taking down a Burmese Army slave labor patrol and losing Jack and David to land mines just before the crossing. Just before crossing back into Northern Thailand with the liberated Pawkinyaun, he thought now. You never cried before on a mission but you wept that night. Freed those farmers and their children and lost two good men and saved forty-three people. They never knew a day of slavery again in their lives. And now they are free. Crossing the Salween before sunrise, river darker and somehow more beautiful than you'd ever seen it before. September 2nd, 2001. And nothing harder, he reflected now, than telling Jenny and Sophia that Jack and David were dead.

Tommy wept now and shook his head and wiped his tears away, looking up at Jesse.

"Jack and David were brave, Jesse. Your friends were very brave. They saved those people and they stopped the bad guys. You had great friends, Jesse, you really had great friends."

Jesse nodded to him and smiled, saying, "Roger that, buddy. That's mighty kind of you, Tommy. And you've got a great teacher in Mrs. Scofield, she's teaching you the right way to live. And you're right about my mom, God bless her. Tommy, you're right, once my mom got into heroin, she was on the way to an early grave and I reckon she knew that, too. But what I want you to remember about my mother, more than anything else, is that she loved me because she saved my life, in her way, in the only way she could. She knew the priests and the nuns would take care of me, she had faith in them taking care of me. Every year on Mother's Day and Father's Day at the orphanage, well I hated those days, I hated feeling so alone and so damn sad. But the priests and nuns at the orphanage, Tommy, they loved me. My mother, God bless her, was right about them. She was so right to have faith in them. They taught me so much, so many good things. They taught me to stay away from drugs, too, just like Mrs. Scofield is teaching you. They taught me to give charity to others less fortunate than me. They taught me to follow the way of Christ. And they taught me to never feel sorry for myself, to never feel like the world owes me anything. The world doesn't owe us anything, Tommy. They taught me to believe in myself and to never say die, to never quit and to never give up on myself. And I know that losing Billy, it feels like you just had a piece of your heart taken away, like a piece of your heart was cut right out of you, doesn't it?"

Tommy looked right at him, his eyes welling with tears, and reached out and hugged Jesse again and he was crying now.

"You felt like that, too, Jesse?," Tommy asked. "You felt like you lost a piece of your heart, too? That's how I feel every day now since Billy died. Every day. Every day it hurts. I want to make it go away but I can't. I can't make it go away."

Jesse nodded to him, picking up his axe now and gesturing toward the cut pine.

"Every day, Tommy. I'll tell you what, I feel like that every day, too, like you, but not all day long. Just for a little while, not even a minute, between sunrise and my first cup of coffee. And I say a prayer right then, when I feel that sadness come over me, when I see the faces of Jack and David and everyone I ever lost at war and everyone I couldn't save. I pray for their souls and their spirits and I pray to God a prayer of thanks. A prayer of gratitude. The truth is that you can't make it go away until you accept that it won't go away. That pain, that sorrow, that sadness you feel is a part of you now. You've got to accept that part of you that's changed forever, that pain is just a part of your life now. It's a very strange thing but it is real, as real as that hawk in the sky and as real as the wind in the pines on this mountain: Once you accept that pain, once you accept that pain as part of you, you won't feel it eating you up anymore, you won't feel it hurting you night and day. And you've gotta' be grateful for being alive. Just for being alive, just for waking up and breathing and simply being alive. There's joy in being grateful for being alive, Tommy, incredible joy. There's joy in being alive. Every day when I watch the sun rise, I feel good to be alive, to see the beauty of the sun and to feel good about the day to come. And I feel the same way looking at the stars at night, it feels good to be alive and see the beauty of the stars at night. It really does. Billy would want you to be happy in this world, buddy, he would want you to go on and live your life and enjoy your life and get your dreams."

Tommy stood up now, axe in his right hand, watching the hawk soaring slowly in the cloudless high blue skies north of them.

"I've gotta' be grateful for what?," Tommy asked, looking in his eyes.

Jesse looked at him.

"For being alive, buddy," he said slowly to the boy. "You've gotta' be grateful for being alive. Do you want to live every day, and be happy about being alive?"

There were tears in the boy's eyes now. He clenched and unclenched his fists, looking at Jesse in the snow on the mountain. I wish I could make it all good again, Tommy thought, biting his lower lip and looking down, I just wish I could make it all good again. He looked at the mountains and he thought how strange it is that the world can be so beautiful and so sad all at the same time. Now he looked at Jesse and wiped the tears from his eyes.

"I want life to be like it was before Billy died," Tommy said softly, looking Jesse in his eyes.

Jesse took a knee, not losing his eyes. O Christ what do you tell him, he thought now. What do you tell this kid who is hurting in a place deeper than you ever hurt. You can't lie to this child, my Lord he has the saddest eyes but you can't lie to him, he's got to face it. Facing it is how you got through, thanks to the priests and nuns. Father Ben and Sister Cecilia and all of them. Facing it. And it will hurt him but there's no other way. No other way to get to the other side of the mountain. O Lord, he thought, praying in his heart, O Lord be with Tommy, be with him now. Don't lie to him, brother. Lord be with him now.

"It's never gonna' be that way again, champ."

Tommy looked away, his head down, crying now.

"Look at me, Tommy," Jesse said now, "don't look away, look in my eyes."

The boy turned his face up, looking in Jesse's eyes.

"Wipe those tears off your face," Jesse said.

Tommy was shaking now and crying again.

"You love your mom and dad, don't you, Tommy?"

"Yes I do and they love me, too, Jesse, I love my mom and dad, I really do," Tommy said quickly, snot running out of his nose and tears pouring down his face. He pulled out his bandana and wiped his nose and his face and looked Jesse in his eyes.

"They love you very much, don't they, buddy?"

Tommy nodded to him.

"And Father James and Becky, they love you, too, don't they, Tommy?"

"Yessir, they do, and I love them, too. And I love James Taylor and Carole King, too!," Tommy shouted, a tear rolling down his face.

"All right then. It feels good to be alive and to know that your mom and dad and Father James and Becky and James Taylor and Carole King love you, doesn't it, buddy?"

Tommy nodded to him and grinned and shouted, "Yes!," smiling and crying, tears rolling down his face now.

"It feels good to be alive right now and feel this wind on this mountain and see those hawks over the trees, doesn't it? Are those hawks beautiful, Tommy?"

Tommy looked at the mountains and the sky now for a spell and he looked west at the sun over a distant mountain. He could see three hawks flying west, black wings beating in blue skies. Looking in Jesse's eyes, he nodded to him and he was no longer crying.

"Those hawks are beautiful, Jesse. I hope Billy is in heaven. Can Billy see the hawks and the sun and the blue skies and the moon hiding behind the clouds at night, in heaven? I would like that. I would like for Billy to see the hawks and the sun and the moon in heaven."

"Billy can see everything we can see in heaven, Tommy, he just sees it more peacefully and he's feeling no pain, there's nothing but peace in heaven, nothing but peace and love and hawks and the sun and the moon and the stars and flowers, all the time."

"Can Billy listen to James Taylor and Carole

King in heaven, Jesse, can he do that?," Tommy asked, folding his arms.

Jesse smiled, saying, "You're damn right Billy can listen to James Taylor and Carole King in heaven, buddy, 24/7, night and day, heaven wouldn't be heaven without those great songs by James Taylor and Carole King. Every time James Taylor and Carole King sing those great songs, they bring a little bit of heaven to us here on earth. Now, can you do me a small favor, buddy?"

Tommy nodded to him.

"Pray with me."

"OK, Jesse."

"Just repeat what I pray, all right?"

"OK, Jesse."

"O Lord, thank you for the gift of life," Jesse prayed, his eyes closed.

"O Lord, thank you for the gift of life," Tommy repeated, closing his eyes.

"O Lord, I am happy to be alive," Jesse prayed.

"O Lord, I am happy to be alive," Tommy said.

"O Lord, I pray for the spirit and soul of my good friend Billy," Jesse prayed, speaking slowly, wind dusting snow on them. He could hear the faint call of ravens south of them on the mountain.

"O Lord, I pray for the spirit and soul of my good friend Billy," Tommy prayed, his voice strong, nearly shouting out the prayer now.

"O Lord, may Billy rest in peace, O Lord be with his spirit and soul always, he was a good boy and we miss him and love him, always," Jesse prayed now, the wind dying down.

"O Lord, may Billy rest in peace, O Lord be with his spirit and soul always, he was a good boy and we miss him and love him, always," Tommy prayed, speaking each word slowly and softly.

"O Lord, be with Billy's family always, be with them in soul and spirit, be their rock and salvation, guide them and protect them on this journey of life," Jesse prayed now.

"O Lord, be with Billy's family always, be with them in soul and spirit, be their rock and their salvation, guide them and protect them on this journey of life," Tommy prayed.

"O Lord, be with my family always, be with us in spirit and soul, be our rock and our salvation, guide us and protect us on this journey of life," Jesse prayed.

"O Lord, be with my family always, be with my Mom and Dad and my double-Uncle Hank and Granddad and Grandma, be with us in spirit and soul, be our rock and our salvation, guide us and protect us on this journey of life," Tommy prayed. "And be with Jesse and James Taylor and Carole King and Father James and Becky too, Lord!"

"O Lord, be with me always, keep me safe from

all harm, guide and protect me on this journey of life," Jesse prayed now and Tommy repeated the prayer, looking at Jesse now as Jesse took a knee and looked him in his eyes, a sober look on Jesse's face, his eyes kind and cheerful, looking at the boy.

"Mighty kind of you to pray for me and James Taylor and Carole King and Father James and Becky, buddy," Jesse said, looking at the boy and giving him a thumbs up. "Many thanks."

"I didn't want to leave anyone out, Jesse," Tommy said, smiling and looking him in his eyes. "I reckon I should always pray for all my family and all my friends too, and even people I don't know but it's good to pray for folks you don't know—Father James said it's good to pray for folks you don't know."

Jesse nodded to him and reached out a hand.

"Yes it is. Feels good to be alive, doesn't it, champ?"

Tommy shook his hand, nodding, looking Jesse in his eyes.

"Yes it does, Jesse," the boy said, nodding his head slowly, "it feels good to be alive. I like that saying, I'm gonna' write it down when I get home tonight. It feels good to be alive."

Something in his eyes now, Jesse thought, something in his eyes that wasn't there an hour ago, something strong and real and calm. He's got a ways to go, Jesse reflected now, but he may just be coming around, God bless him, he may just be breaking on through.

"Jesse," the boy said now, looking at the mountains and the sky, "I can see the hawks in the sky and look at the sun and tonight I can look at the moon with my mom and dad. I like looking at the moon and the stars at night. The moon is always changing but the stars stay the same. Life changed me like life changed you."

Jesse nodded to him, looking in his eyes.

"But now life is what I make it. Life is what you make it, you said. Now my life is what I make it. Life is what I make it. Is that right?"

"That's right, champ," Jesse said, patting him on a shoulder.

"Roger that, Jesse," Tommy said, grinning and wiping a tear from an eye. "I guess I can't make it like it was before Billy died, can I Jesse? I can't make my life the way it was then. Life changed me like life changed you. Everything was more beautiful, then, when I looked at the mountains and the sky, there was a beautiful feeling inside whenever I looked at the mountains and the sky. Billy is in heaven now and I hope he can see us on this mountain. And he wants me to be happy, too. That was a good prayer, I liked that prayer. It made me feel good, praying to feel good to be alive. It's OK to feel good to be alive, isn't it, Jesse?"

Jesse smiled and looked him in his eyes.

"Yes it is, Tommy. Always. It's always OK to feel good to be alive, buddy. Now, can you do me another small favor?"

"Sure," Tommy said, his eyes bright.

"Let me tell you a story."

Tommy nodded, "Is it one of your stories, Jesse?"

"Not exactly, buddy," Jesse said, "It was one of David Storm's favorite stories. It's from a Buddhist temple, in Northeastern Thailand, from a place called Loei. It's a true story, about a man who saved a woman's life in 1994. David Storm told me this story in 2001."

"Man, that's an old story, Jesse, that's from before I was *born*."

"That's right."

"And the man saved the woman's life! Wow. That's beast! Did he pull her from out of a burning car or a motorcycle accident or something, Jesse, was he a fireman or a policeman?"

"No, Tommy," Jesse said, smiling at the boy and looking in his eyes. "Don't get me wrong, buddy, I want you to know that firemen and policemen are brave and saving people's lives is part of who they are and what they do. The man wasn't a fireman or a policeman, though. And she wasn't in a fire or an accident. She was a farmer's widow, a young woman who wanted to take her own life."

Tommy squinted.

"You mean she wanted to kill herself?"

Jesse nodded to him.

"Who was the man, Jesse?," Tommy asked. "Who was the man who saved her life?"

"He was a Buddhist priest, Tommy."

"And the Buddhist priest saved her life! So was he a priest, like Father James is a priest?"

"Not exactly the same, buddy, but much the same. Not so different. Buddhist priests wear orange robes, and sometimes black robes like Father James if they are Zen Buddhist priests. It's not the color of the robe but it's the kindness and compassion of the priest that matters, Tommy, whether they are Buddhist or Catholic. And the priest in this story, well, he is very much like Father James, in truth."

"Great!," Tommy exclaimed, clapping his hands. "Please tell me it, I wanna' hear it."

"Tommy, there was a young Buddhist priest in Northeastern Thailand, near the Mekong River. The priest's name was Phra Suchai. The farmer's widow, her name was Chalanee and her husband had died three months before, in March 1994, in a motorcycle accident. He was nineteen and she was seventeen and it broke her heart. They had a little daughter who was a year old and just a baby, of course. The woman came to the Buddhist temple in the middle of the day and all of the other Buddhist priests had gone to study, at a Buddhist college up the road. Phra Suchai was the only priest at the temple and the woman told him, "I'm glad you are here, I came here to tell one of you to tell my mother and father that I was a good daughter and that I loved them, because I will die today." She wanted to kill herself, Tommy, that's how sad she was about losing her husband in that motorcycle accident. The priest kept her in the temple, praying with him but she still wanted to kill herself, after many prayers. And he saved her life, he kept that woman from killing herself by telling her that her daughter had already lost one parent to a horrible accident that no one could really explain, just a tragic terrible accident, but if she took her own life, her daughter would lose the only parent that she still had. And Phra Suchai told the woman that suffering and pain and heartache come to all people in this world, he told her that we all suffer in this life and we must accept that pain, we must accept the pain that comes to us when we least expect it and never want it, accept it and carry on, accept it and keep on living with faith and hope and love for a brighter day. She wept and cried then, Tommy, the farmer's widow wept and cried and told the priest that she'd never thought about her daughter, only about her own grief and she stopped crying and the priest called her mother and father to come and help her. And her daughter grew up in that same farming village, with her mother right by her side. That mother is still alive today, Tommy, and her daughter is nineteen now."

Tommy nodded to him, something like acceptance there in his eyes now, Jesse thought as he split another chunk of pine and heard the boy chopping wood near him.

"I like that story, Jesse! That man saved her life, that's a great story," Tommy said as he slammed his axe into a chunk of oak. "Jesse, I gotta' ask you a question. Is it always hard like this?"

"What's that, champ?," Jesse said, chopping wood.

"Life. Is life always hard like this, Jesse?"

"Not always this hard, buddy. But sometimes, yes. I'd be lying to you if I told you otherwise. Jack used to say, "Life is hard and love is forever." That was his motto, you might say, that was his creed. It's always hard losing your friends, Tommy. It always hurts. And you want to hit back but you can't hit what you can't see."

"Only me can help me. Like you told me, "Only you can help you." Life changed you like life changed me. I like what Jack said, too, Jesse. Life is hard and love is forever."

"Roger that, champ," Jesse said, chopping wood. "And only you can help you. You've got to help yourself. You take that first step and it's terrifying, I know, it's like walking into the unknown. Because you are walking into the unknown, when you're walking out of pain back into life, knowing that life is going to hit you again. It's like walking out of the shadows into a sunrise. There's some comfort in the shadows, the comfort of knowing your surroundings. It's easy to stand in the shadows, isn't it?"

Tommy nodded to him, setting his axe down, holding it by his side, his eyes glistening with tears.

"You know, a beautiful ship looks beautiful when it's in port, on a calm, still day, no wind and the sun is shining and beams of light reflect off the brass fittings," Jesse said, setting his axe down too, hope in his eyes as he looked at Tommy now. "But a ship never looks more beautiful than at high sea. And the high sea can be dangerous for a ship but the high sea, the wild, wide-open sea, Tommy, is the most beautiful sea in the world. A ship is made for high sea, Tommy, a ship is made for the dangerous seas and the beautiful seas and the calm waters, too, and everything in between. God made us strong, Tommy. God made us strong enough to handle the dangerous times in life and He gave us the courage to face death, if need be, and the faith and the hope and the love to love one another, to help one another, and to save peoples' lives, even the lives of complete strangers. We're not built for the shadows, buddy, we're built to cross mountains and seas and deserts, God gives us the strength to journey and to reach for our dreams. A ship isn't made for a port, Tommy. A ship is made to go to sea. So are we. We're made for the sea, we're here to go to sea, come what may. More than anything else, as Father James has likely told you, we are here to love and to be loved. And sometimes life is this hard, as hard as what you're dealing with, losing Billy. Losing your best friend in the worst way, watching him die right next to you."

Jesse reached out a hand to him and they shook hands and Tommy nodded to him as if to say go on.

"Life came at me hard, Tommy. But love is real and love makes you feel good to be alive, for all the pain in life. You can take the pain if you believe in love and believe in yourself. And your mother and father love you very much, and so does Father James and so does Becky. I hope you get your dreams, buddy. Well and truly, I hope you get your dreams. But you'll only get them, you'll only dream your dreams in the first place, if you believe

in yourself. Believe in yourself, buddy. Go the distance. Believe in yourself. Only you can help you.
Only you can believe in yourself and carry on. I
think Billy would have wanted you to do that, to
carry on and dream big dreams and go to sea and
get your dreams. I think Billy would have wanted
you to be happy, Tommy."

Tommy reached out his arms and Jesse hugged
him and patted him on his back.

"Jesse, how long were you a Ranger?"

"Long enough to know when to leave," Jesse
said, grinning. "Six years, buddy. Six good years,
all told. Now chop up those old pine branches yonder and those chunks of oak, chop them up good."

Tommy nodded to him. He could see his parents and Father James and Becky out on the porch
of the cabin now and they had mugs of steaming
hot black coffee in their hands and there was smoke
coming out of the chimneys of the mountain cabin
and he waved to them, smiling.

"All right, Jesse," he said, looking at his parents again and at the priest and his wife and they
waved back, smiling at him.

"Good," Jesse said, turning and waving to Cole
and Vickie Benson and to Father James and Becky
and smiling at them.

Looking at Tommy now, Jesse took a knee.

"OK, buddy. First half hour of each training

day, we're chopping wood," he said, looking in the boy's eyes. "So that's the next thirty minutes, chop it up good. Chop wood for four minutes at a time, without stopping, nice and steady. Rest two minutes, then get to chopping again. We'll do that for a half-hour. Once you get used to that, after a few days, we'll move it up to five minutes at a time, turning big pieces of wood into little pieces, and so on. You want some more hot chocolate?"

Tommy nodded, looking at him, his eyes brightening.

"Good, we'll have some after we're done chopping wood," Jesse said, handing him an axe. "And I want you to know something, Tommy. You are never alone. There is always someone to reach out to. Every time someone reaches out to you, there's a bridge there, between you and them. That bridge wasn't there before but it damn sure is now. And that's a good thing, a beautiful thing about life, because every time you build a bridge to someone, or they reach out to you and build a bridge to you, well, you're making new friends. There's real treasure in friendship. What I'm saying is, don't be afraid to build those bridges, Tommy, and don't be afraid to let people build those bridges to you."

"It's good to build those bridges, I guess, isn't it, Jesse?," the boy asked, folding his arms. "Your friends, like Jack and David, they built those bridges to you, didn't they? That's why you were able to save the children. That's why you were able to break those chains and kill the bad guys. I'm sorry that Jack and David are dead, Jesse. I'm sorry for Sophia and Jenny, too. Sophia and Jenny must miss them. I know that Billy would be sorry for them too, if he was here, I know he would. What do you do when it hurts, though, Jesse? What do you do when you remember them and it hurts?"

Jesse winced and thought, man he has been there, he has been there right in the heart of it, God bless him. O Lord, Jesse prayed now in his heart, O Lord be with this child, be here now.

"There's times I just stop, buddy," Jesse said now, speaking softly to the boy and looking at him with calm and cheerful and kind eyes in the mountains north of Chinle, "the memory of my friends comes back to me. And I feel that sadness, Tommy. And I say a prayer for their souls, for their spirits and I carry on. They would want that for me, Tommy, I know that they would want that for me. They would want me to carry on and live with a whole heart, really *live*. I know that Billy would want that for you, too. He was your best friend and I'm sure he would want that for you. But *you've* got to want it, Tommy. Only you can help you. You can't live in the hurt locker for the rest of your life. And know this, we are all here for you. All of us. You've got a friend, buddy, you've got a friend in all of us. Now, could you do me another small favor, Tommy, if you don't mind too much?"

"Yes," Tommy said quickly, his eyes bright, looking Jesse in his eyes.

"Pray, every day, a prayer of thanks and gratitude for being alive. Like we prayed today. Make that prayer every morning, when you get up. Can you do that for me?"

"Yes I can," Tommy said. "Can we pray again tomorrow, like we prayed today? I reckon that we're gonna' chop wood again tomorrow. We can pray again tomorrow and chop wood and tonight I will listen to James Taylor and Carole King with my mom and dad and I'm gonna' tell my dad to play the James Taylor CD on the stereo in his truck today, too, when we go back home, that's what I'm gonna' do, Jesse. My dad has a real nice stereo in his truck!"

"Roger that, buddy," Jesse said, smiling, looking in the boy's eyes. "Now your dad has a Carole King CD too, right?"

"Yes he does and my mom has one, too, she has a Carole King CD and Becky has a lot of them, Becky has lots and lots."

"Good, well, have your mom play some Carole King tonight before you go to bed, too."

Tommy nodded and said to him, a reflective look in his eyes now, "Do you pray every day for your buddies who died, Jesse? Do you pray every day for Jack and David?"

"Every morning, buddy. And I pray for the people we could not save, there were some people we could not save and I pray for them, too, I pray for their spirits and their souls. Every morning, Tommy, I see their faces—"

"—Like I see Billy's face every morning?"

Jesse put a hand on his shoulder and looked him in his eyes, nodding to him and thinking, walk with him, Jesus, walk with him, Holy Spirit, walk with him, Blessed Virgin Mary, walk with him all the angels and saints, Lord, be with him now.

"That's right, buddy. That will always be true and you just have to accept it. Be glad that you knew Billy, be glad that you were blessed to know him, blessed that he was your best friend. That's how I remember my buddies who died with me at war. I'm glad I knew them, I'm glad that I was blessed to know them, that I was blessed to call them my best friends. And I carry on, just like you're carrying on. You've gotta' carry on now, Tommy and live every day with joy for every sunrise, for the hawks and the mountains and the sky and with joy for the fact that you've got a great mother and father and damn good friends."

Tommy reached out a hand now, a sober look in his eyes, Jesse thought as he shook hands with the boy.

"You remember your friends who died at war that way, don't you, Jesse, with the prayer flags?"

Jesse nodded and wiped a tear from an eye and smiled at him.

"Roger that, Tommy. Roger that. I remember my friends who died at war with me that way, buddy. Their spirits are always with me. I pray for them and for their loved ones, every day. And every day, I pray gratitude to the Almighty, a prayer of gratitude for being alive. Have you prayed for Billy's family, since he died, the way we prayed for his family today?"

Tommy gritted his teeth and shook his head.

"No," he said, looking down.

"You don't have to feel sorry, buddy," Jesse said, "you got hit by a tsunami and when you get hit by a tsunami, hit by a tidal wave, your whole world falls apart."

Tommy looked up at him now.

"I will pray for Billy's family tonight, Jesse, I will! I will pray for them. And tomorrow morning I will pray for Billy's family and every day I will pray for them. And I will pray for Mrs. Scofield and for Alice and for everyone in my class, too.

Jesse, what does it mean, when you said you pray for the spirits and souls of your friends who died at war, what does that mean?"

Jesse smiled, looking at him.

"Well it means this, Tommy, I close my eyes and say, "Lord, may my comrades rest easy. May the love of Christ be with them. May the healing power of the Holy Spirit be with them. May the blessed love of the Virgin Mary be with them. May their spirits and souls be at peace. May their service and sacrifice never be forgotten. And may we meet again on higher ground, no rifles or sidearms or fighting knives or grenades in our hands anymore, just good women and good whiskey and good music, let the good times roll. Amen. Jack had a saying, Tommy: *God understands.* God understands our pain like nobody else. God understands *your* pain like nobody else, Tommy. God is with us when we lose our loved ones, our families and our friends. God is with us in every hard time and every good time and every in-between time. And God is with us now, here on this mountain. God is love. God understands, buddy. And when I pray for the spirits and souls of my friends, my comrades who died at war, I know that God understands, I can feel His peace and His love and His understanding. And there's another prayer I pray every day, every morning. I pray a prayer of thanks for knowing those brave men who were my best friends. I pray to the Almighty, "Lord, thank you for blessing me with the friends I knew, the comrades I was blessed to serve with." They were my best friends, Tommy, like Billy was your best friend."

"And you remember them with the prayer flags, too," Tommy said, reaching out a hand.

Jesse smiled, looking at him. He shook his hand and gave the boy a thumbs up and slapped him on a shoulder.

"Roger that, champ. I carry those prayer flags with me wherever I go, to honor their memory. To honor them. They were good men, they were brave men and they died trying to save lives. I know that they would have done the same for me, if I hadn't made it. Buddy, let's chop some more wood while the sun is still shining. I think Jack Dempsey would approve of us chopping wood in Northern Arizona, don't you think? Would Jack Dempsey chop wood in the snow, buddy?"

Tommy laughed, slamming his axe into a chunk of pine, the bark flying off as the axe blade bit into the wood.

"Roger that! I reckon so, Jesse, I reckon that he would approve. He sure was a wood-chopping man, that Jack Dempsey. Jack Dempsey chopped wood, chop chop chop! Jack Dempsey chopped wood, chop chop chop! Jack Dempsey was heavy-weight champion of the world and he chopped wood! He was tough. And I can chop wood too, just like Jack Dempsey. And I can throw the stones out of the pit like Rocky Marciano! And I can run in the snow like Joe Frazier! They were boxers, Jesse! I'm gonna' be a boxer, too. Can I ask you a favor, Jesse?," Tommy said, smiling as he chopped wood now under the winter sun, sweat beading on his forehead.

"Go right ahead, buddy," Jesse replied, nodding to him as he split a chunk of pine. He was praying a Hail Mary in his heart for the boy as he grabbed another chunk of pine under high blue mountain skies and he was feeling no pain and he realized that for the first time in his life since he'd left Northern Arizona in September 1988, he really felt at peace in his heart and soul.

Tommy set his axe down, looking Jesse in his eyes now.

"Can you show me how to make a prayer flag for Billy?"

"Damn straight, champ," Jesse said, smiling, slamming his axe into a tree stump. "We'll do that today."

"Roger that, Jesse!" Tommy said, a smile lighting up his face.

"We'll chop some more wood, buddy, and put some fighting gloves on you and hit the heavy bag," Jesse said, "then I'll show you how to make a prayer flag for Billy. Father James made twenty-six prayer flags already, for all the kids and teachers, all the people who were murdered in Newtown, Connecticut eight days ago. I reckon you'll see all those prayer flags at Midnight Mass, he told me he'd be putting them up outside the church on Christmas Eve, Tommy."

"They were first graders, like me, Jesse," Tommy said, raising his axe and slamming it into a chunk of pine and splitting the wood. "And you know what, Mrs. Scofield said we must never forget them! Mrs. Scofield told us that American children need to have the right to go to school and come back home alive. And I told my mom and dad what Mrs. Scofield said and they agreed with her, they did, they liked what Mrs. Scofield said. I cried, Jesse. I cried when Mrs. Scofield told us in school that all those children were dead, they were just little kids like us, just first graders. Mrs. Scofield told us that those kids at Sandy Hook Elementary School had their whole lives ahead of them and that bad man stole their lives, just stole their lives. I don't want anybody to come into my school and steal my life, Jesse."

"Neither do I, Tommy," Jesse said, chopping

wood steadily, chunks of pine and oak piling up near him in the snow.

"What were you doing when you found out about all the first graders like me who were shot down at Sandy Hook, Jesse? Were you chopping wood or something, or were you in the jungle with the tigers and stuff? What were you doing? I guess you were in Penang. I was in school and Mrs. Scofield was teaching us math tables and two times two equals four, that's what I was doing."

"I was looking out to sea," Jesse said, looking in his eyes. "You're right, buddy, I was in Penang. I was drinking coffee in Penang, Tommy, looking out to sea. I've got bamboo on one side of my house and a small field on the other side and boulders beyond the field, near a beach. I was drinking coffee and talking with my neighbors on the other side of my bamboo. You can see the ocean real beautiful there, you can see the Strait of Malacca all blue in the distance. My neighbors are Chen and Vivian Loh, they're Malay Chinese and their people came from Southern China a long time ago to Penang. There are no more tigers on Penang, buddy, all the tigers got hunted out over a hundred years ago on Penang. But there's still plenty of jungle, just raw, wild jungle, on the western side of the island, facing the Strait of Malacca. Chen and Vivian were drinking tea and I was drinking coffee and their daughter, Melanie, came crying out of the house and they rushed up to her and she fell into their arms crying. Her mother walked her back into the house with her arms around her. And Chen, well, he's a good old friend of mine, he's a lawyer and I've known him and Vivian for fifteen years now. And he walked over to me with tears down his face and told me, "Twenty-six of your people have been killed at Sandy Hook Elementary School in Newtown, Connecticut, Jesse. First graders and teachers and staff. I am so sorry, my friend, I am so sorry." I cried too, buddy. I wept. And I felt ashamed, Tommy. I truly felt ashamed."

Tommy looked at him and said softly, "Why did you feel ashamed, Jesse? Why?"

"Because it was my duty as a Ranger to defend Americans, to protect our people and our homeland, Tommy. It was my duty to save American lives. It's shameful, to me, what happened at Sandy Hook. Nothing but shame. In the rest of the world, kids go to school and enjoy being alive at school, don't even think about getting murdered at school."

Jesse wiped tears from his eyes.

This is his world now, more than ever, Jesse thought. Tommy and kids like Tommy, they are the future. My God I hope they live to see the future. God protect them, God protect Tommy and the kids here. Just kids here just like those kids at Sandy Hook, just teachers trying to teach kids to live good lives and learn their ABCs and just teachers helping kids build their futures. Just kids. Those kids at Sandy Hook were murdered. Murdered no different than anyone is murdered by Al Qaeda, murdered no different than anyone is murdered by any terrorist. Murdered on American soil just like our people were murdered on American soil by Al Qaeda on September 11th. How many billions of dollars spent on counterterrorism since September 11th and not one dime spent and not one law passed to protect American children in American classrooms.

"And those kids and the teachers and staff at Sandy Hook, they were Americans, Tommy," Jesse said now, squinting, going on, crows' feet etched deep around his eyes. "They were Americans, just like me and you. They were just kids, just kids like you. When I was a kid growing up at the orphanage here in Northern Arizona, Tommy, I was safe. I was an American kid and I was safe. There were no metal detectors at my school. My teachers never had to give us drills on how to dive under our tables if we came under fire at my school. My teachers never had to slide steel over the doors or have bulletproof glass in the windows or doors at

my school. My teachers never had to wonder if going to school one day meant going to school for
the last time, my teachers never had to say good-
bye to their children and loved ones in the morning and wonder if it might be the last time they
ever see their children and their loved ones alive.
I never had to wonder if a day at school would be
my last day on this earth, buddy. I always knew
that I'd walk home from school, not get carried out
of school in a body bag. I was a kid growing up
in America, Tommy, just like those kids at Sandy
Hook growing up in America but I was safe. All
the kids your age at Sandy Hook were Americans,
buddy. They were Americans. They had the right
to live free from terror and free from fear. They
were American kids and they were gunned down
right in their classrooms and carried out of Sandy
Hook in body bags. That would never happen in
Malaysia, where I live, Tommy. It simply would
never happen. We don't carry kids out of schools
in Malaysia in body bags. Buddy, I've got a place
in the mountains in Portugal, too, and I'll tell you
what, we don't carry kids out of school in Portugal
in body bags, either. Melanie and teenagers like her
in Malaysia, and all the first graders in Malaysia,
and all the kids in schools in Portugal, they enjoy
a right that those kids at Sandy Hook never en-
joyed — the right to go to school and come back

home alive, just like Mrs. Scofield said. I want to see America be a place where you enjoy that right, too, buddy. I want America to be a place where kids enjoy the right to go to school and come back home alive. And I hope and pray that you grow up and fall in love and get your dreams and live a long and happy life, Tommy, I truly do. I'm sure Billy would have liked that for you, too."

Tommy nodded to him and there was no sadness in the boy's eyes now. The boy looked at the mountains and the mountains looked beautiful to him and he felt like he was looking at the mountains for the first time in his life and he prayed in his heart now for Alice and all the kids at his school.

"Roger that, Jesse," Tommy said, looking in his eyes. "I think Alice would like that, too, and all my friends. But Jesse, I'm sorry. I forgot something."

"No worries, champ. What'd you forget?"

"I forgot to wish you a Merry Christmas, Jesse! I'm sorry. My mom and dad told me last night to make sure I wish you a Merry Christmas. Merry Christmas, Jesse!"

Jesse reached out a hand.

"Merry Christmas, Tommy," he said, shaking hands now. "That's mighty kind of you. God protect you—God bless you and keep you safe and well, buddy."

"God bless you too, Jesse! Hey, can all my friends make prayer flags for Billy, too? Would that be all right?"

"Absolutely," Jesse said, giving him a thumbs up. "They sure can, Tommy, all your friends can make prayer flags for Billy. That's a great idea."

"Good," Tommy said, peace in his eyes now. "You know what, we go into the second grade next year, right after Labor Day! We'll be second graders and I'll be a boxer, then. Were you a boxer when you were a second grader, Jesse?"

"Yes I was," Jesse said, smiling, "right here in Northern Arizona, Tommy. I'll tell you what, let's put these axes down and put on some fighting gloves, champ. Time to hit the heavy bag."

# About the Author

The only author of his generation compared to Hemingway, Mike Tucker holds degrees in history and literature and honors in poetry. Born in 1960, he was raised in Japan, Northern England and America. Following his apprenticeship as a writer in Washington, D.C. from 1983-86, where he worked as a concrete and demolition laborer, he served on active duty in the US Marine infantry. In 1990, his first book was published, *Unreported*, a work of poetry. *Hell Is Over: Voices of the Kurds After Saddam*, his critically-acclaimed work of history, was a finalist for the Ben Franklin Award in History in 2005. Under fire as a young poet with Spanish counterterrorists in Barcelona in 1981, he was the only author on counterterrorist missions with both Delta Force and SEAL Team 6 counterterrorists after September 11th. His fifth work of fiction, *Clandestine*, a novel, will be released in November 2014. He lives in the Near East and Portugal.

CPSIA information can be obtained at www.ICGtesting.com
Printed in the USA
BVOW01*0111121113

336029BV00002B/4/P